# The Whole Art Thing

# THE
# WHOLE
# ·ART·
# THING

## JUSTIN SPRING

A
Joan
Kahn
BOOK

**St. Martin's Press**
**New York**

THE WHOLE ART THING. Copyright © 1987 by Justin Spring. All rights reserved. Printed in the United States of America. No part of this book may be used or reproduced in any manner whatsoever without written permission except in the case of brief quotations embodied in critical articles or reviews. For information, address St. Martin's Press, 175 Fifth Avenue, New York, N.Y. 10010.

Copyeditor: Camille Schmid

Design by Paolo Pepe

*Library of Congress Cataloging-in-Publication Data*

Spring, Justin.
    The whole art thing.

    "A Joan Kahn book."
    I. Title.
PS3569.P547W5  1987      813'.54      86-26224
ISBN 0-312-00204-1

"A Joan Kahn Book"
First Edition
10  9  8  7  6  5  4  3  2  1

For Moira and Sharon,
and Professor Nick Palermo,
wherever he may be.

# Contents

I would like to thank Professor William H. Pritchard for the good humor and patience he has shown in advising this work. Others who, if less directly involved, were no less significant to its completion are: Rob, Tabitha, Ezra, Claire, Karl, and the three Jameses. No list of acknowledgments is complete without specific reference to Mom and Dad. Thank you, Mom. Thank you, Dad.

Next morning Rossetti did not come down. Hall Caine looked at his library, wandered for a little about the unkempt garden where Mr. Watts-Dunton was "reluctant to interfere with Nature in her clever scheme of survival of the fittest," and left a little before luncheon without saying good-bye to his host. He had a great deal to think about on the train north. A chill had struck into the heart of the young man. Was Art quite such a noble thing as it had seemed in Liverpool?

—Evelyn Waugh
*Rossetti, His Life and Works* (1928)

# PART I

# Vagabond Shoes

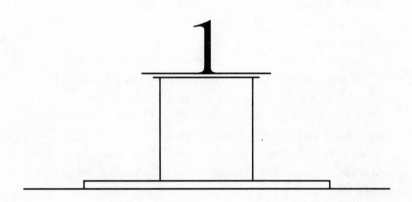

"Art is *easy*, Scooter. Scraping up *lunch* is hard. Your primary responsibility as an artist is survival."

James was lying on the aqua vinyl sofa, staring at the ceiling; at two in the afternoon in the middle of February at Amherst, Joan had called to discuss careers, ostensibly his. She had woken him up. He closed his eyes, sleepy, and fidgeted with the receiver.

"I really need a decent pair of shoes," he said. "I've never had a really nice pair of shoes. Never."

"I told you. Get the wing tips."

"Mmm."

"Anyway, you'll make it. Artists always manage to sell. I'm the one that's doomed. Broadway's *dead*."

He heard her pause, expecting contradiction, but as he was biting his thumbnail he said simply, "Mmm."

"Not really. But sometimes I get scared I'll never make it."

"Make it," he repeated absently.

"Money."

"Artists aren't worth anything till they're dead."

"Actresses?"

"We'll do fine."

"I'm serious."

"I'll do fine."

"No doubt." Silence. "Advertising."

"No way. Come on . . . you know what I mean. Things just work out for people like us, don't they?"

"I'll be a failed actress in Washington Heights, growing old on cat food and Equity newsletters."

"No way. Not so dramatic. You'll have three kids, tuna casserole, community theater, and a husband who commutes."

"I'll do the commuting, thanks."

"Okay."

"And I happen to like tuna casserole."

"There you have it."

He tugged at his underwear, listening to the silence on the other end of the line. "I'm depressed, Joan."

"Not again."

"Well, it's not every day that your favorite professor commits suicide after class."

"It's good you can talk about it. I'm sure it wasn't anything you did."

"I suppose," he said, pausing expectantly nonetheless.

"We've been through all that before, a million times. I don't think I can help you much . . . don't you have any interesting problems?"

"I wish. LSAT's Saturday . . . not like I've studied or anything."

"You're no lawyer, Scooter."

"Easy for you to say. You've never met my mom."

"You need to say it more. She drove up in a borrowed Alfa Romeo last homecoming. I met her then."

"Oh."

"Stop being depressed. It's irritating."

"Okay."

He sat up, preoccupied and slightly dizzy. His hair stood on end; the mirror opposite reflected a pleasantly menacing countenance. The room was dim, the day cold and drizzly, and below his feet, the carpet rife with sandy dirt and paper scraps. Stubby and Francis would be home soon. It was somebody else's turn to vacuum.

"How's the application going?"

"Hmm?"

"Deadline."

"Today? "

"One hour. *Scooter*."

"*Okay*. I can probably make it. C'mon over in a half hour and we'll drop it off. It's almost done."

"All right. Just remember what I said. Pull every punch."

"Okay. 'Bye."

The phone clicked. The room seemed suddenly large and still; he rose to look out the window. There was no coffee. There was never enough money for good coffee. And this kind of day required coffee; even the day needed help getting started.

Below, dirty snow stood melting in clumps; puddles stood still and unchanging. The large patches of mud that had replaced the stained and trampled snowbanks in the past few days gave the quad a mottled, scrofulous appearance; caught between definite moments of "weather," solitary people walked from building to building in oddly mixed clothing with varied collegiate looks of distress and exhaustion. A squirrel screeched in the fervorless afternoon. The world needed a good cup of coffee.

Across the quad from James, in the brightly lit offices of the fine arts department, all was snug and cozy. African violets bloomed in profusion on the sill. Unobtrusive classical music played softly on a forgotten clock-radio. Mr. Coffee was on his third brew cycle of the day.

"Yes, he was black in the face, with the tongue sticking out like a carrot. . . . It was on the night of the midterm cocktail party. That would be Thursday. Professor Williams laughed, Professor Hall cried, and while I tried to pull the poor man down Professor Pike remarked from the doorway on our collective resemblance to the Van der Weyden *Deposition*. I believe he had been drinking."

"*Deposition*? You can't mean . . ."

"No, nothing of the sort. The body was fully clothed. The college photographer took pictures, as a matter of fact."

Mrs. Lillian Gilder arranged pastel-hued petit fours with crisp Prussian accuracy as she spoke. A woman of resource and high moral fiber, she had run the department for twenty-two years as its secretary, and departmental suicide, devastating to some, had worked no visible effects upon her physiognomy. She placed two pink cakes on a saucer for Lydia, brought the heaped platter to the conference room, then returned to her desk, and her own coffee, black. There, her reading glasses rose and fell with the sighing of an ample bosom, rising and falling with characteristic forbearance, resignation, and the simple satisfaction of another job well done. Today Lillian had done much: the bimonthly departmental meeting was also a reception for the suicide's widow, and the sideboard groaned accordingly with hors d'oeuvres and hard liquor.

Lydia Platz, youngish art librarian on her coffee break, sat with legs crossed in a large brown wing-backed chair alternating questions with bites of cake. Neither she nor Lillian would attend the reception, as they were staff.

"In his own studio?"

"Yes. He spread a dropcloth. There was no mess."

"Mmm. . . . Awful . . . did he leave a note? These are really *very* good."

"Not to me," Lillian replied rather too abruptly. "Thank you . . . I made a special trip to that wonderful place in Northampton."

The librarian watched carefully as Lillian sat, somewhat flushed, adjusting a marking on her desk calendar; then licked a bit of frosting from a nail with her small pink tongue and blinked, a slight smile playing across her curved lips. Inclining her head toward the conference room, she asked, "What will they do?"

Lillian raised an eyebrow cautiously. Her glasses rose and fell. "I think Blunt will want a memorial exhibition before the widow can leave with the paintings. That should fill our visiting artist slot for the semester at minimal cost. The department may purchase a few of the canvases to offset funeral expenses as well."

The room fell silent; Lillian again made a notation upon her desk calendar. The handsome, self-absorbed professor, so natty, so prompt in reshelving his own books and meeting with advisees, would certainly be missed. Yet Lillian, and even Lydia, had missed professors like him before; for this was a department notorious for what was euphemistically referred to as "high turnover." Few of Merisi's type lasted long; yet in the history of the department never had there been so breathtaking a departure. They had loved Dick Merisi and would miss him, for he had been handsome and caused

7

a great scandal. There was no question in either woman's mind as to who had been its cause, so that when, several minutes later, Professor Pike stalked in, larger than life, to check his mail, it was to the curious and observant silence of both women.

He stared intensely and for no particular reason at Lydia, who met his gaze solidly though not without an inward quiver. He looked different, she thought, but for all that not a bit remorseful.

Satisfied that no mail had arrived, the graying, slightly bug-eyed professor swept a hand through his close-trimmed hair, turned on his heel, and stalked purposefully out. His tense, rapid manner gave him an air of professorial vitality successful with the younger set; but during this, his fourth mail check of the day, Lillian had not looked up from her paperwork. His rapid entries and exits were highly routine.

The office fell silent once more as Lydia alternately flipped through the latest copy of *Réalités* and stared out high windows at the neutral afternoon. At last she rose to leave, wrapping her remaining cake in a napkin embossed with the college seal. Lillian waved a silent good-bye from the phone.

As the click of the librarian's heels receded on distant parquet, Lillian received no answer and hung up. The office was empty and would most probably remain so for the rest of the afternoon. Even the fellowships application box—free money!—sat conspicuously bare. On days like this, days when there were no students, no curiosity, no Art, only the mail, the gossip, and the endless party preparations, what could be done? Nothing, really. This was the fine arts department, the department that always had been and always would be, for better or worse, as long as Amherst was a liberal arts college; a small and dutiful and notably unpopular department, remarkable only for the pleasant situation of its offices.

She sighed; the reading glasses rose and fell on her wide bosom. She would lock up early and go for a sauna today, a long sauna. Tomorrow would be better. Her towel sat reassuringly close, rolled tidily at her feet in the space below her desk.

Professor Pike reentered his magnificent office at the end of the hall. The room was large with an exceptionally scenic southeastern exposure, conservatively furnished with austerely impressive objects, most noticeably cast-iron bookshelves and a great oak desk. The room bespoke an exquisitely subdued artistic temperament, strongly yet unobtrusively tasteful. He had spent many years decorating it just so. Seating himself, he resumed his perusal of *Art Journal,* May 1968. His cold blue eyes gave a look of serious and engaged observation, reminiscent, he liked to think, of Holbein's *Sir Thomas More.*

He stared this way for a reason, for he knew he had an audience. Today, as every Friday, Professor Williams sat in the far corner of the room, palette in hand, a small easel before him, painting Professor Pike's portrait. Which was by no means unusual; they were the closest of friends. In the past seven years Williams had completed twice as many portraits of Pike. Ostensibly he did them for practice: at least, Pike had never offered any sort of payment. Now, as always, Williams, chewing his cigar and sitting on his stool, looked savagely, ferociously puzzled. A fat man whose bohemian convictions apparently prohibited showering with any regularity or conviction, Williams was, despite seeming incongruencies, the confidant and buddy of a trim, dapper historian. Politics had made them bedfellows; vanity and a mutual love of professional basketball explained the rest. Maintaining through the years a friendship that kept the world at a distance and themselves high on a notoriously narrow tenure track, they spent afternoons together no less cherished for their frequency; Pike, with his art historian's gift for colorful description and exacting commentary, would usually carry the conversation while the gruffly oversensitive Williams provided him with a perfectly docile hunk of audience.

While remarkably compatible, neither was today in very good form. This was the fourth professor they had disposed of, in some way or other, in the past three years, and rumors of an administrative shakedown had been about all week. An assistant curator at the museum had that morning presented a sworn affadavit to the dean of faculty proving beyond doubt that Pike had bought the rope, and Williams the dropcloth.

The artist now dabbed irresolutely at a crusty patch of blue upon his palette. Pike looked up, saurian eyes fixed and attentive.

"Don't paint, Rob. It can't be as bad as that."

The professors giggled. Neither had done much of their own work lately; as Williams had cleaned up on an opening held over homecoming weekend, selling two years' work in one drizzly and intoxicated afternoon, he could call the day his own. Yet he seemed troubled.

"I know it isn't," he said. "It's just that those Merisi canvases are going to skyrocket. I wish we'd bought before— well, you know what suicide does for a reputation. If he gets discovered now they'll give him ten pages of *Art in America* and a retrospective at MOMA. . . . It's just not *fair*."

"Mmmm. To tell the truth, I just put in a bid myself. The wife wasn't going to consider it but she's got those expenses to meet. If I get one I'm sure my investment will triple within the year. I plan to talk to her today at the reception."

Williams meditated on his own painting, chewing ferociously on his unlit stogie.

"They're *okay*," he said. Pike had never spoken to him of buying art.

"Fine . . . fine. But the woman is something completely different. I don't look forward to our talk in the *least*."

"Her shoes."

Pike groaned expressively, and they giggled again.

Back across the quad work conditions had deteriorated considerably. Dana "Stubby" Tunbridge and Francis Stonington Lodge II sat together on the sofa recently relinquished by James, idly bouncing lacrosse balls against the wall over his typewriter. James was typing steadily, still hopeful of making the deadline. Lillian had just called to check on his progress, and to remind him to return a studio key he had borrowed. Francis, who had answered the phone, could not understand how his own roommate, once so amusing at punch parties and fraternity initiations, could be receiving calls from the administration at three o'clock on a Friday afternoon, when the cocktail parties had already started. James had declined comment to continue with the application. Besides, he liked talking to Lillian, and was rather proud she would call him. Stubby and Francis sulked together, observing the effect of close-pounding lacrosse balls on the nerves of their erstwhile friend.

From below came soprano protestations of a freshman being dragged toward the cocktail party of her choice. Hysterical laughter occasionally gave way to yips of pain or annoyance. The voice was altogether familiar.

"Carol," said Stubby.

"Up to no good," said Francis.

James nodded. Carol had gone out with him for the last two months, but she was unimpressed with artistic interests and openly deplored his quitting the lacrosse team. James had sat on the bench for three years. Stubby and Carol, never close friends, were now getting on astonishingly well.

The lacrosse balls continued to pound with a slight irregularity.

"Wonder where Carol's going," said Francis. It had been a slow afternoon.

"Cocktail party," said Stubby.

"Wanna go?"

"Mmmm . . ."

Outside, the mist had grown thicker; festive sounds wafted up through still air. Rock music, the tinkle of a smashing bottle, the halfhearted cheers of the work-worn on a Friday afternoon; above all, snatches of Carol's voice, delighted coloratura. The icicles on the eaves dripped dully; James noticed with some pleasure that his reflection in the slightly fogged windowpane had grown stronger in the failing light.

The pounding had stopped. A door slammed, followed by cleats descending. He sighed and bit his thumbnail. No one had wanted to vacuum; the room was dreary, and the quiet so longed for during the week was no consolation now.

In another fifteen minutes James had finished the application; he rose to see Joan marching across the quad, her hitop galoshes sucking and crunching deliberately through mud and snow. Bundled in woolens, red knit hat low on her brow, long brown hair trailing into the hood of her snorkel parka, she was, from this distance, small, childlike, angelic. He retrieved the application from the murk of his desk, sighed looking at it, and joined her below for the walk to the fine arts building.

Joan was considerably larger and more intimidating at close range; if anything, more seraph than cherub. She stood now on the landing looking up, radiant with the cold and her own peculiarly appealing irritation.

"Happy hour," she said.

He raised his eyebrows.

"The boys at the Phi just dragged Carol past my window. She was harmonizing on a lacrosse cheer."

Her galoshes squeaked fiercely on the stone as she approached. She was smoking a cigarette. "You'd think she'd go out and play the game herself."

He looked down, nodding. "She likes it."

"You're not still . . ."

"Nah."

"So what's wrong?"

"I don't know. She is. Everything."

He felt her touch his arm, and looked up to encounter a gaze of profound and concerned intolerance.

"What?"

They stepped out of the dorm onto the soggy quad.

"The suicide . . . I just feel like there's no room in the world for me or what I want to do."

"Ridiculous. There's always New York. Are you talking about anything specific?"

"The suicide note . . . you saw my copy. That note. The note said it all. There's just no room anywhere. There's just no *place* for it. Don't you remember what he said? It was so moving . . . so awful."

"It was okay."

They walked on in silence. Before them rose the fine arts building, originally a physics laboratory, staid, solid, beautiful in an otherwise jumbled landscape of ersatz Colonial mistakes. The building was the first done for the college by a world-famous firm of architects, and the only one at the college they'd ever got right. Modeled on a Renaissance palazzo in red-brick (cornice, pediments, and entablatures faced in delicate terra-cotta, the brickwork decorative but simple),

**13**

fronted with a beautiful and eminently practical Romanesque arcade, the structure radiated integrity, an industrious beauty rosy with health in the weak winter sunset. Sort of like Joan, James occasionally thought, and sort of like Mrs. Gilder.

"So what's the big problem, Scooter? Let's run through it and tell me if I've left anything out: existential despair, fear of death, legitimate grief overshadowed by apprehension of your own future. And Carol. Is that it?"

"I guess."

"You're wiped out. That's fine. Everybody is. If you need help you could see a shrink. You can see them for free right here. It's on the health plan. It won't cost you a cent."

He shook his head.

"Church?" she said dubiously.

"No . . . it's not that . . . The problem is that I'll never make a living even if I'm good at what I do. The whole art thing looks like a big fat dead end."

"Shut *up!*"

James looked at her, then around at the buildings on the quad, then down.

"Maybe you can say that in thirty years, Scooter. *Maybe.* but you can't expect me to take that sort of thing seriously till then. Understood?"

He nodded, feeling better.

"Can I see the application? You should've worn socks."

He handed it to her. She flipped hurriedly through the several essays describing his personal background and career plans.

"Growing up poor works nicely . . . good understatement but you're right there with the facts. And the independent from an early age bit has to go over well. This looks really legit."

They entered the building just behind a woman in heavy mourning, sniffling quietly behind a dark veil.

"Good inclusion of varsity sports. I hear they really eat that stuff up. There are a lot of typing mistakes, but I think that kind of works, too—artistic temperament implied by flawed grammar and punctuation. Very nice."

The application was on time and accepted. James expected more of a fanfare than he got; almost everybody was in the seminar room at a reception. Only Professor Pike loitered outside, chatting with Lydia by the plaster reproduction of a funeral stele sided by potted palms.

While locking up the office, Lillian offered James and Joan homemade cookies sprinkled with vanilla sugar. The three left together, but then Lillian had to run back to fetch her towel.

They paused, waiting for her on the long elegant staircase, its steps indented by a century of ascending and descending feet, munching ruminatively.

"You want to go for coffee?"

She looked at him, surprised.

"I'll buy."

"Gee . . . sure."

James rarely bought coffee, even for himself, but it had been that kind of day.

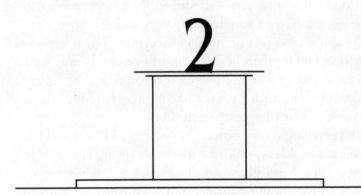

"We have to talk about your study habits, Scooter. You can't afford sleeping till three."

"I can afford everything. Let's go shopping."

"Nobody likes a lazy artist."

"All artists are inherently lazy," he said, yawning, ". . . and they thrive on dislike."

Switching the receiver to his other ear, he reached for his coffee, which was the good expensive kind. He had received his fellowship.

"Come shop with me."

"Sounds *thrilling*."

"Shoes," he said meaningfully. "Plus I'll buy you a Snickers."

"Save it. We'll never get there before closing, you and your swelled ego lying around in shorts."

"We'll make it fine, babe."

Silence. He knew she detested the word "babe."

"Watch it. Hey, I heard there was a party at your place last night. Sorry I wasn't invited, or I might even have *come.*"

He groaned, then threw his head back over the armrest, a sofa pietà. The sticky couch creaked. He had not known there would be a party, and moreover wished there hadn't been; the room was a mess. Stubby and Francis, in hosting an impromptu lacrosse team gathering, had relied heavily upon his nude figure drawings for decoration and entertainment. Those that remained on the walls bore glyphs and slogans; others had become hats; several were used as hand towels after an accident at the punch trough; even as he spoke the room played host to a flock of tiny animals, precisely folded newsprint accented with stray marks in nu-pastel. An industrious exchange student had stayed up all night making them.

He had been only slightly dismayed by all this; he didn't need the drawings for a course or anything, and he could certainly always draw more; he had just thought them nice. Looking at it philosophically, he enjoyed the paper animals. But then again, Carol had slept over with Stubby; the roommates had left early for a lacrosse tournament and she, after making coffee and leaving a note promising to help with the cleanup, had disappeared as well. Perhaps she had gone to watch the game.

"Inez said she saw the Stubby-Carol thing a mile off, but didn't know if you knew so didn't want to say. Anyway, how's the work going? Have you even stopped by the studio lately? I think you might make more of an effort. Have we got a date for tonight . . . the opening, I mean?" She paused, and receiving no response said, "Scooter?"

He stirred, noticing for the first time the spilt punch. "Huh? No. Not really. I don't know. It's all these trashed nudes."

"Who?"

"Nude drawings. All my drawings have been made into kitty litter."

"Oh."

"And I keep bumping into Mrs. Merisi carrying shoeboxes of stuff out of the studio. I introduced myself, you know."

His thoughts wandered. The conversation had been short, eulogistic, humorless: He had hoped she was doing well; she had hoped his work was coming along all right. The professor had mentioned him to her several times.

"She's leaving this week. De-pressing. Oh, the weirdest thing. Pike sent me a totally bizarre note."

He sipped his coffee, looking down at the few sentences Carol had scribbled. "I'm not going out with her, but does she have to sleep with my roommate?"

"Who? Oh. It's her decision."

"It's my room."

"And Stubby's. How are those guys, anyway?"

"The haircuts? Fine."

They now had identical haircuts, part of a team psyche effort. James had done the same the year before.

". . . They don't talk to me much. I suppose I used to do that sort of thing."

"Not convincingly. What about the note?"

"It's been pretty lonely here."

"Right. The note?"

"Hmm . . . oh, I don't know. It was to congratulate me, but it seemed to imply I owed him something for it. I suppose I do. I threw it out. It was depressing."

"You didn't write back?"

"He'll be there tonight. You're still up for it, right?" Walpurgisnacht, the Merisi retrospective, was opening that night at the college's art museum.

"Anything for quality cheese and an open bar."

James sat up with furrowed brow. "C'mon. You know his stuff is amazing."

"I guess. You're the artist."

"Anyway, Lillian said tonight is mostly pâté. Are you still up for that shoe-shopping?"

"Two guesses."

"Ten minutes."

He yawned once more, then said a quick good-bye.

A half-hour and a brisk walk later they stood, Snickers-in-hand, before the nicest shoe store in downtown Amherst, Mathews' Shoes. Joan knew Frank Mathews personally, and called the store "Frank's Shoes" to bring up the subject whenever possible. Entranced by shoes, she had metamorphosed at the prospect of selecting footwear. Her ruddy cheeks glowed, her eyes grew clear and enormous; her windbreaker flapped quite stylishly open behind her, and she wore her favorite loafers, normally reserved for the most special occasions, in honor of the imminent purchase. James knew they were making their first appearance of the year—she had told him— and felt appropriately honored.

"We're no slouches," she had explained as they walked arm in arm, stepping gingerly past puddles and mud on the town common. "Frank notices what you wear. He knows his shoes, no question."

James had frowned for a moment at his own dingy running shoes, worn, rain or shine, for over a year. They did not impress. But he had also worn his very best pair of socks, merino argyles, his little brother's Christmas present of two years past. Despite their present incongruity, he remained confident of their ability to please, and said as much to Joan. At her insistence he knelt before the store to tie the same laces he would momentarily untie.

"It's good manners."

She had not bought shoes for over a year herself.

They walked into the store together, and were there greeted by the warm, dry smell of leather polish and tissue paper. James breathed deep and perused one of several display tables while Joan said hello to Frank. He had risen at their entrance, perhaps to greet her.

A tall, thin-haired man in his late thirties, he wore a double-breasted jacket, maroon tie, and gray stretch slacks. His shoes were brown and plain but completely appropriate to the workplace. Joan had spoken excitedly of him on the way over, for she liked him very much; now, standing before her, he seemed the embodiment of respectable mystery, vastly superior to any college boy.

Joan, whose passion for shoes was in large part the reason for James' imminent purchase, had made a point of introducing herself to him in her first hours at school; she was also the first to speak to him in depth, to find out that he was a bachelor, a university graduate, played on the local softball team, occasionally took roles with the Valley Light Opera Company, and drove a silver LeMans Town Coupe.

Upon provocation Frank now spoke briefly of his vegetable garden. Joan listened intently.

"That's great, Frank. . . . Won't the asparagus be in soon? So early? That's probably right around *Hedda Gabler*. Yes, that's right. Hedda. I hope . . . in English."

She shifted from one leg to another, pointing one toe before her, coquettishly caressing the nap of the clean beige carpet.

Frank smiled in Joan's direction and stared out of the window at the bright day, then went away briefly to ring up a purchase. Then they both joined James at the display window.

"How can I help you?"

James stood transported, eyes glazed, shoulders slumped, mouth slightly ajar in a way both friend and salesmen understood intimately. This was the ecstasy of potential shoe ownership, commonly known in the trade as "shoe fever."

Joan poked him.

"Oh. I'd like to . . . buy shoes."

"I see."

"We'd like to see these and these in an eleven-and-a-half," Joan said hurriedly. "Right?"

Frank nodded and disappeared behind a curtain while they argued in hushed tones over the relative merits of the two pairs she had picked, their posture and expressions recalling Dutch genre paintings in which cavalier and barmaid haggle raffishly by fading sunlight.

"Now *this*," Joan said with a slightly quivering eyebrow, "may just be the new you . . . the look is hot, young, artistic."

James considered, his eyes shining.

"Maybe too much of a statement here."

"You'll definitely grow into it. The look comes first, then the explanation. Don't be afraid."

"Aren't they kind of . . . expensive?"

She tilted her head provocatively.

"You've got the check, Scooter."

They had indeed deposited the check for one thousand dollars from the Friends of Fine Art the day before, together, at their bank—receiving, they preferred to think, VIP treatment from Bonnie DiCola, by far the most desirable teller. Bonnie had raised her plucked eyebrows in surprise, made a mysterious phone call of negligible duration and, after a suspenseful moment, spindled the check with gusto. James had for the first time dared to take a candy from the dish she kept at her window. Joan agreed afterward that it had been a great moment for all involved.

"You need flash, Scooter. . . . You saw the *Times Magazine*. All the best artists get their start wearing the hottest shoes. The rest comes naturally."

"Dick Merisi didn't."

But it was too true. Last week's *Sunday Times Magazine* had settled the question. In a survey of the Hot New Abstract Expressionists, each picture in the fifteen-page full-color spread had featured artists in interesting shoes of some sort or other. One Expressionist had even appeared in black tie and opera pumps. Joan had kept the picture on her door for weeks, but spoke equivocally of the artist, whose name was merely "Sancho."

"He's awful," she had said. "Nobody puts on black tie in midafternoon."

But these shoes were something else entirely.

"Grow, Scooter. Put yourself into these shoes. I *know* shoes. These are the shoes of the artist."

"That's so superficial."

"Life is superficial."

"You're superficial."

"And better for it."

But his passion was fading with her insistence; the moment, once so promising, was upon them, and no longer his to treasure alone. He looked at her with sudden determination.

"You're no authority. There's much more to being an artist than new shoes. It's a moral issue."

"Don't you believe it."

Frank had silently reappeared and now sat lacing the new pairs at a distance from the arguing couple. "Would you please remove those," he said, pointing tentatively at the running shoes.

James did so, placing them behind his chair to accommodate Frank, who now approached wielding shoehorn and stool before him, as if for protection from animals. James was glad that he had worn the argyles; so, he hoped, was Frank.

He tried the shoes that he had preferred first, which had little chance under Joan's withering gaze. Frank stared impassively beyond the shoes and out of the window. Even the shoe mirror could give no assurances, for by a trick of perspective, just above the left toe, Joan's head rose Medusa-like in its expression of horror and disgust. He took the shoe off at some distance from her and gave it silently to Frank, who promptly interred it with its mate in their paper-lined box.

Next came Joan's choice, which was, in fact, extraordinary. Fine hard leather, thin and smooth as a tiny seashell, it squeezed his foot with reassurance of good things to come. The embrace at the instep was all arching restraint, the kiss of a lady dressed and powdered for luncheon. As he stood and walked, each shoe gave the impression of a wayward beauty, polished and diffident, relying on him only for their locomotion and a situation in which, Narcissus-like, each might dally perpetually before its mirror image.

"Wow, Scooter . . . it's even better than I thought."

In the mirror Joan's head hovered once more, now beaming like a baroque putto. Her opinion notwithstanding, James knew the shoes changed his posture slightly, made him stand taller, somehow more attractive, more interesting. They would help him hold his own in conversation, make him look more at ease, but keep him from getting lost in the crowd, which was a problem he had.

"Well?"

"Yes, yes, yes," he said, doing a little dance in his new and slippery-soled shoes.

"Wrap them up please," said Joan, then adding, her surprise tempered by instant taste and good manners, "Isn't that Guillaume Brix-Webber staring at your purchase?"

Indeed it was. Guillaume, also known as Gill, diminutive leader of the off-campus scarf-and-spectacles set, stood outside the window, leaning close and fogging the glass. They waved to him immediately and with pleasure. Gill was the most visible and most reticent of Undergraduates Worth Knowing. He dressed exceptionally well.

As he entered Joan said, "Gill! Just the person we were wishing would walk in the door!"

Gill walked forward sheepishly, unwinding his scarf. He was short and bundled and his spectacles had fogged on entering.

"Hello, Frank," he said.

Frank nodded.

"Hello, Joan-and-James," he said slowly, with a vague smile.

He came over and stood quite close to them both, wide-eyed. James knew he had contact lenses but rarely used them, preferring spectacles instead for their mandarin élan.

"You're buying shoes," he said, smiling warmly.

"You bet. C'mon, sit down."

Joan quickly whisked James' coat from what had recently been James' chair, crossed her legs, and contentedly struck a match. Frank moved off behind his curtain with a preoccupied look. James remained standing for a moment, watching her light her cigarette, then looked down for a moment at his shoes and sat on Frank's low stool facing his two friends.

"Have you heard of James' fellowship?"

Gill shook his head, eyes opening wide and expectant.

"It's *wonderful*."

She sketched in the details. James nodded, occasionally offering the odd correction.

Gill looked visibly impressed, much more so than James would have suspected. He was, in James' opinion, one of

24

those people who seemed to know and appreciate everything, the successful product of metropolitan education and exorbitant wealth. Enormous privilege and a strong sense of self made him genial, confident, and well rounded, if occasionally difficult to take seriously.

"And what are you wearing?" Joan said with a barely suppressed smile. "It's not quite Japanese anymore. We haven't seen each other for so long. . . . Where do you *hide* yourself?"

Gill shrugged. He was wearing heavy gray overalls from the People's Republic of China; hi-tech Japanese, he explained, was a phase long behind him. His eyes opened wide with delight that she had noticed, however. He explained briefly that he had been working hard for the past month at a soup kitchen around the corner from the shoe store.

"After all," he said with great conviction, "there are lots of hungry people in Amherst, too."

Joan nodded with enthusiasm. James went, "Mmm," looking down again at his shoes.

"So does that tie in with the overalls?" Joan asked.

"Sure . . . I dress down, other people dress up, and we meet in the middle. It's very simple."

Joan's mouth fell open in admiration and she nodded, then laughed.

Gill looked at James, and, pushing back his spectacles, said, "I'm glad you're buying those, by the way. I was tempted myself, for quite a while. Are they still on clearance?"

James looked, and nodded.

"Shoes like that need a very special wearer. . . . I'm sure they rest on capable feet."

"He knows," Joan said, in reference of course to Gill.

"I'll do my best with them."

Gill smiled.

"Are you coming tonight, Gill?"

"To the opening? Yes, of course. I'll be there. It sounds truly sordid, what with all Lydia's told me about the department. For one of the smallest on campus it has quite a reputation."

"The art itself is quite something, though."

"Were you a student of his?"

James nodded.

"It wasn't all that bad for James, though. He was depressed for a bit, but then he always is. We talked about it forever. You know, he's getting an A in the course he was taking, no questions asked? And I hear the widow leaves sometime next week by bus."

"I didn't say anything about a bus."

Gill nodded. "She hasn't said anything to me about it either."

Joan looked at him in surprise, then stubbed out her cigarette with a preoccupied look.

"Now I have the fellowship in any case," James eventually said. "It's helped me feel considerably better. But I'll never forget Dick Merisi. . . . He was the man who first showed me what Art really was."

"*Is,*" Joan corrected.

"And now you're buying shoes with the money for the fellowship," said Gill, his puzzled look fading to one of delight.

James nodded, thinking of his former professor's scuffed oxfords. "Life goes on."

Gill bit his lip and nodded, wide-eyed. "We should talk about this fellowship sometime soon. You really must come and live at my house this summer. I live in New York, you know."

Joan started. She had heard fabulous stories of the Brix-

Webber house on Fifth Avenue, and once even managed to stop by, unannounced, to see what it was really like.

"I used to, uptown," James said. "Now my mom lives in Riverdale, which is in the northwest corner of the Bronx, near Yonkers. It's not really like living in the city, though. See, my mom got mugged. So as soon as she started making money she began moving to better neighborhoods."

Gill looked a little confused, but said only, "You should definitely live with me. . . . We need people like you in our house."

"Like what?"

"Artists."

"Oh."

"My mother's always wanted a real artist in the family—how's Carol, by the way?"

James' sad story followed. Gill nodded sympathetically. Frank returned, sales slip in hand, holding as well a plain brown package for Gill. They decided to speak again at the opening that evening. Then Gill invited Frank to the opening. Things changed hands. With some prodding from Joan, James introduced himself to Frank. The shoes were wrapped and boxed and the running shoes were put back on; these too attracted the notice of Gill, who admired them for their lived-in quality. Coats and scarfs were gathered and donned; the three left the store in high spirits with the bell on the door tinkling merrily behind them. The door shut, and the fresh blast of cold spring air dispersed among the silent shoes. Frank shut the register and returned to his stool with a heavy sigh, staring out as feet passed briskly on the twilit pavement.

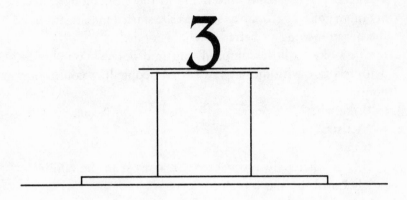

# 3

James had always been adept with crayons, Magic Markers, and construction paper; he had always liked drawing and making things, and did a lot of it in classes to keep himself amused. But he only began to call it Art about a year before winning the fellowship, and only at the tentative promptings of a much-admired professor, for he knew he was not what might be described as a "natural." In high school, sports and grades had meant too much to become involved in Art, but as an unremarkable double major in Art and English, he had had plenty of free time at college. Moreover, in the crowd he traveled with, fine art had a presumed chic; his friends saluted his endeavors with pleasure, if from afar. They did drama or music, and each seemed to do something particularly well. For that reason, perhaps above any other, James felt compelled to do something artistic as well. Since he could not act, sing, dance, or tell stories, his choice had apparently been made for him. He specialized in printmaking and applied for the fellowship. When his award was announced he threw a party his friends had long anticipated, at which they laughed, danced, sang, acted, told stories, and agreed once again how lucky he was.

As a student he showed promise but not ambition; drifting from course to course, department to department, he seemed interested and entertained by everything, but happy as well to sleep late, spend an afternoon with the crossword, or sit up nights reading unassigned novels. He made a point of not setting priorities or making lists. When exam time came, he would stay up night after quiet night, drinking coffee and eating biscuits alone, writing spirited if mediocre papers and generally enjoying the change of pace. After exams ended he would celebrate. While his professors liked him and his friends liked him and he was generally regarded as an interesting, intelligent, and cheerful person, he did not impress anyone very much. Most of the time that seemed just fine; where his artistic ambitions lay he did not know, and finding them immediately did not seem of particular importance. He would find something. He supposed he could go into advertising, and said as much to anyone who asked.

He was good at printmaking and liked his professor very much. He also found it to hint at a life he would like to lead: one of making messes, working hard, and creating things that looked nice. He liked looking at pictures, browsing in art supply stores, touching different papers, using pencils, reading bulletin boards. Carrying a portfolio had a cachet all its own, and going barefoot in the snack bar was something only a studio major could do. Besides, he liked having something to show for his work. He sent much of it home to his mother; some of it she framed.

But when friends left and dorms emptied and work put off

was finally done and in, James was usually the last to leave and the least excited by prospects of departure. With nothing to do and nowhere to go and no plans for the future, he spent the final days of the semester leafing through folders in the career-counseling office, sipping Cremora-laced coffee from a small disposable cup, and thinking what a big, cold, empty world it was outside. All his friends seemed to have everything planned; as he poked alone through pamphlets describing the rigors of fine art, he entertained the idea of a life in advertising. Eventually, though, he would spend another summer washing dishes and reading novels, taking informal art classes at a nearby community college, enjoying himself as best he could alone. He was nearly always broke.

One day early in his junior year a Xeroxed announcement came from Lillian saying that the Friends of Fine Arts summer fellowship for the practice of studio arts, a grant of a thousand dollars, would be awarded by the department to one of its majors. James was taking two studio courses that semester, and so skipped the business breakfasts and interviews, worked very hard, and kept his ears open. Something like this was just what he'd waited for; a fellowship in Art sounded like a picnic.

The previous fellowship winner had held her opening a few months later. She had done very little with her thousand dollars and her work was not good; James attended her show with a keen interest and left, not concerned with his own abilities so much as sure he could win the prize. Joan encouraged him, though she had not gone to the show.

"I know you can, Scooter," she had said. "No one else will try."

"True enough, but unimportant," he had replied gallantly. "The prize is within my grasp."

"And I'll come spend weekends in your loft and we'll go dancing at all the hot places to see and be seen."

That had sounded like just the thing. But a subtle change was overtaking James, one that had disturbed their relationship and changed his life. He became what Joan somewhat disparagingly referred to as "*l'artiste sérieux*," a state under which his perceptions of the fellowship and life in general had been somewhat too zealously altered.

That summer Dick Merisi, the new printmaking professor, had arrived at the college; he was an excellent and industrious teacher and artist; he taught both James' studio courses. A relationship developed of the sort that misty-eyed parents will often recount to their children as The One Good Thing That Made Their College Worthwhile. It was that for James. By the end of the semester, after passing up parties, football games, a number of picnics with beautiful women, he really was, for better or worse, an aspiring artist.

Under these new conditions of existence, receiving the fellowship was a less thrilling affair, no longer a serendipitous diversion so much as a challenging opportunity.

"That means work, Scooter," Joan had said in the snack bar. "What a drag."

The work was fine; but a good deal of worry came along as well. What to live on and how to succeed, worries that had overwhelmed James even with his previous lowbrow aspirations, now became a matter of decimal-point statistics and late-night stomachaches. He had never met an artist who was not a professor, and, frankly, he doubted they existed. He had one old friend, Marina, who was reputedly attending art school in New York, but as she had always been of the sort that transcribe Joni Mitchell song lyrics with colored pencils in math class, he wondered what his inclusion with her in a career subgrouping could possibly mean.

And then, on top of all that, Merisi had, after a semester of quiet agony at the hands of the department, done himself in for reasons never quite made clear. In his conversations with James he took a dim view of the art world, intimating that there was no possible place in which an artist might exist to work other than academia. And academia, as revealed to James through Merisi's eyes, was nothing to aspire to. Professors Williams and Pike had had something to do with the final days, James knew, but some deeper despair had guided his hand as well. The Xeroxed suicide note had said as much.

Then there was Joan to consider. Freshman year he had thrown in his lot with her and he had not been sorry; while Art had kept him busy, she had made him happy. She encouraged him in his work but did not pretend to understand it; as the semester progressed he had seen less of her and more of the studio; while he liked the studio well enough, he missed her terribly, apparently more than she missed him. She was drifting.

So he thought as he walked back from dinner beside her. They had just agreed, after ugly disagreement, to meet at his room after the Joyce seminar pizza party. She was going to the party. He was going to his room.

Before dinner she had changed into a black dress with a red pin, matching the worn softcover *Ulysses* she carried at her side like a clutch purse. The pizza party was an event she had long looked forward to, roughly an equivalent for her of James' dead professor's art opening.

"Only literary," she was quick to add at dinner.

It would no doubt be a difficult evening. In part because of something James had said about Gill on the way, and in part because Joan said something about Carol to change the subject, and also because they had had too much good coffee that afternoon, all the joy and pleasure of shoe-shopping had rapidly disintegrated over a fried fish dinner at Valentine. The whole thing began when James had wondered aloud how much like death a stomachache could be, because he had a stomachache.

"Don't expect anything from me tonight, Scooter," she had said, dragging on a cigarette. "I really can't deal with you."

He then told her he hated when she smoked at meals, which had done little to ease postprandial détente.

But then, over coffee, she was very beautiful in her black party dress; with her face all powdered and lipsticked, she startled him. She looked sophisticated. Exhaling smoke in the heavy, odored air of the dining hall, she seemed to have mastered an uncomfortable situation, and with her long legs crossed she looked very comfortable indeed.

Her jealousy about his living in New York came as no surprise; for three years they had lived through each other's triumphs and failures, neither exhilarated nor distraught, but only jealous and supportive by turns. In fact, nothing about her could surprise him and very little about her irritated him for long. While the corners of her mouth might be turned down farther than usual tonight, the mouth itself, even painted bright red, was naturally, wonderfully beautiful, and quite worthy of his appreciative contemplation.

James recalled, sipping bad dining hall coffee, how they had once actually "gone out," and the discomfort engendered by what was to both of them a surprisingly touch-and-go relationship. They had decided quite rationally and with little silliness not to jeopardize their friendship; they had gone out with others since, but never for long and never with conviction, at least not on James' part. Their peculiar bond, passionate in temperament, platonic in practice, had withstood hormonal inquietude as statues withstand the elements, developing a patina, a cozy green crust that, colorfully absurd, was nonetheless a fine and distinguishing attribute. The whole arrangement was a superficial eccentricity of something still, solid, monumental—satisfying to think on and appreciate for what it was, most of the time.

Since they were not in love, and since he was rather expecting it, James did not brood over her jealousy; he hated her for a moment, then felt sorry for them both. She deserved a break like his, and he deserved better from her, but after all she really didn't mean to act the way she did, and in her place he would probably carry on the same way.

He sipped again. "Want to stop by after?"

No. She did not much relish the idea; he should meet her after instead.

"It's on the way, isn't it?"

She hated climbing the stairs.

"You climb stairs to visit Inez all the time."

What did he want?

"Nothing. Forget I even asked."

That had been at the dining hall; they had been silent since. The wider spaces and happier smells did them both some good, so that when they parted at his dorm entrance they were once more friends, and she would come up the stairs to his room after all.

Her faint, twilit smile flickered in three-quarters profile, then disappeared up the path to the chapel where the pizza party would be held.

James turned and entered the dorm, wondering what the evening would be like. Dinner had been foul; his stomachache persisted; walking toward the dorm he had seen that his room lights were on, which was not necessarily a good thing. But as he climbed the stairs the abstract idea of possibilities, an idea quite independent of Joan or himself or his artistic abilities, loomed large. He was on his way somewhere, both tonight and this summer, and from this distance it seemed very exciting.

The dorm was hot and stuffy after the damp, earthy spring air outside. From the basement came the rhythmic thump-and-humming of the laundry room; above, a hall phone rang, and doors slammed in unknown places at odd intervals. The B-side of *Born to Run* played, as it did each night, for the reclusive chem major in the suite across the corridor.

Stubby and Carol sat in the social room, side by side on the sofa. Stubby read the *Times*. Carol knit, the yarn resting comfortably in her lap. They were listening to classical music on the Norton Scores, for pleasure.

"Hello, James."

Handel mingled with Springsteen and the regular sliding click of Carol's needles. He stayed for a moment to discuss that evening's parties, then slipped away on the pretext of folding laundry.

In the bedroom he changed and sat alone in his good clothes, drawing caricatures and writing postcards. He read a letter Marina had sent him about being an artist in New York, describing a performance-art/fashion show held at Danceteria for Tibetan orphans, and how last week she had shaved her head, and how she was living with a lesbian photojournalist for the *East Village Eye* who hated cats. It cheered him up enormously. During the time before Joan arrived, the classical music drifted from Handel to Mahler, investing the too familiar Springsteen from next door with an orchestral Sturm und Drang that was not unappealing. The sound in fact seemed to approximate his growing sense of the next room's activities and the evening as a whole.

At last there was a knock outside and the sound of voices. The record began again, at Pachelbel's Canon in D.

"Walpurgisnacht," Joan called through the door.

James opened, feeling natty in his art-opening clothes. On occasions when they were both dressed up, as now, they often kissed. It was a sort of ritual. They kissed. She tasted like pizza.

"You can leave *Ulysses* if you want."

"No way . . . don't you think?"

"Hmm."

"It goes."

"Have a good time," Carol said. "You both look very nice."

They emerged from the dorm holding hands, and with a sudden blast of cold wind he felt her shiver and move closer. The wind had risen after sunset, and low clouds, visible in the sky-glow of the Hadley greenhouses and the Route 9 mall complex, threatened rain.

Once out on the quad they were surprised to meet, heading in the same general direction, two vaguely familiar outlines. Frank Mathews and Gill were walking together toward the upper quad, speaking about something that sounded like aesthetics. Joan hailed them; they waited; soon the two couples joined and said hello. Gill was wearing a flight mechanic's jumpsuit and a large silver hoop in his ear, while Frank wore coat and tie, the tie different from that he had worn at work in the afternoon.

"Hi"

"Oh . . . crap. My wallet," James said. "I better go back."

"I'll come along," Gill said.

Joan took Frank by the arm. "We'll wait at the snack bar in the fine arts building . . . you like beer, don't you, Frank?"

The walk back to the dorm was mostly silent.

"Did you know about Frank Mathews?" Gill asked. "He's an artist. We're trying to fix him up with my family's gallery connections in New York. We're good friends with Rupert Boynton of Boynton-Crest."

James nodded, interested, as Gill explained that though Frank's art could boast no real social significance, he liked him very much as a person. "You should talk to him, James. He's a very interesting man."

James promised to start a conversation of some sort that evening. "I like Frank," he said. "Very much."

That made Gill happy. Then James ran up alone to fetch his wallet, but as it was in the bedroom and the door was closed, he seemed to have to borrow money after all.

Gill waited down on the steps, and smiled vaguely, as usual, while James explained his predicament.

"Of course," he said. "Beers are on me."

But as they recrossed the quad, his expression seemed to change, and he leant closer to James, in fact shouldering him off the path and into the mud several times.

"I've been meaning to ask you something . . . you won't mind? This seems like the right time—"

"What? . . . Excuse me."

"I wanted to ask about your specific thoughts on the role of Art in contemporary society. Picasso says that 'painting is not done to decorate apartments; it is an instrument of war for attack and defense against the enemy'—don't you agree with that?"

There was a strange gleam in his eye as he said it. They walked on in silence.

"I'm a printmaker, you know."

"Yes, of course . . . in the tradition of the Ashcan School and the WPA."

"Did Picasso say anything about etchings?"

"I'm not sure."

"He made *tons* of etchings. Picasso was one of the most

successful modern printmakers. But it *is* the sort of thing that ends up . . ."

"Come to think of it, I believe we have two. You don't work abstractly, do you?"

James felt somewhat embarrassed. He had never really tried; it was not the sort of thing that any of his professors had ever encouraged in him.

"Well—"

"No, no—that's good. I've always felt myself that the world needs artists who deal with the realities of the human condition. Art shouldn't reach only a limited coterie of aesthetes."

"Sure."

"I mean, you don't necessarily compromise aesthetic responsibilities when you produce a work that can profoundly affect the common man, do you? You agree with me there? And *I* think that with your unusual social background you're just the sort of person to promulgate change in the world of contemporary art. This is very exciting for us both. You'll be coming in from the outside, you see. . . . At least, that's my impression. We'll develop a populist art. Art and soup. I have great expectations for you."

The campus looked and smelled very beautiful; the dark trees against the cloudy sky, the lighted windows across broad expanses of muddy turf, the brisk and chilling air that swept them along toward the snack bar reminded James of a ferry trip he had once taken by night from New London to Orient Point, staying on deck the whole way. It was one of his favorite memories. In his mind he was there.

". . . Under the present state of capitalism," Gill said, "the position of the artist is hopeless. Nothing he does reaches anyone outside a limited and powerless coterie of aesthetes. As an artist you'll have to face the realization that you've cut yourself off from all serious activities of life. I know—you think that making art is serious. To you, maybe. But to the world, not really. Not at all, in fact." He tapped James on the shoulder. "You have no significant place in society. If you wish to have any effect on the world through your work you'll have to take on the establishment. Your art will have to be aggressively political, locating itself entirely outside the context of the present art world. And you can do it all with social realism. It's what you do anyway."

"You mean, drawing people and places?"

"Yes."

"I suppose I do do that."

"It's especially good because you've proposed to do it in decrepit urban areas."

"You mean my old neighborhoods."

"Yes."

They had reached the snack bar.

Joan and Frank had been conversing deeply over beers, and persuaded them to sit drinking a while longer. One beer stretched into four pitchers, and an hour later, slightly tipsy, they left to walk up to the museum. James spoke with Frank about the relative merits of working as an artist outside of New York, and of the specific merits of living in the Pioneer Valley, though he was, in truth, not much interested in the latter. Joan spoke with Gill about the upcoming *Hedda Gabler,* for they both had parts. Gill and Joan walked ahead, talking rapidly, while James and Frank followed behind, their conversation serious and subdued, as befitted the visual rather than performing arts.

The museum rose before them, a dark, formless silhouette against the cloudy sky. It was in many ways a counterpart to the other fine arts building that James liked so much, the nineteenth-century red-brick palazzo whose shady arcades and simple, elegant cornices welcomed art students with secure and well-appointed surroundings as well as its own snack bar. Built by the same world-famous firm as that rosy citadel, the museum was even named after the firm's partner, who had attended the college. Fifty-four years younger, it boasted innovations and conveniences that the original could never possess. Its site and maintenance and facilities were vastly superior. But the building had cost five times more to construct and was arguably the ugliest on campus.

The low, featureless structure commanded the best view of the Pelham Hills that the college could offer, yet had no windows. Although it had been designed specifically as a museum, approached from any direction except head on it resembled either a small warehouse or a large infirmary; the chief feature of the building's north end was its loading dock, which commanded a delightful view of the northeast campus and, ironically, a breathtaking prospect of its old red counterpart at the bottom of the hill. The building's lack of any true architectural detail was made up for by selectively applied white paint approximating neo-Colonial detail; its bogus pilasters, pediments, and border trim peeled, not quaintly, but in profusion, so that flowers near the museum annually died before blossoming, dispatched by the toxic paint chips.

A not unappealing church had been razed on the site in the year of the museum's construction; only its sandstone-and-granite steeple remained, a strange and compelling structure dominating the museum's sunless forecourt. To the right of the steeple stood a sculpted marble entryway by a man named Waugh that, incongruous with both structure and landscape, apparently took for its inspiration the mausoleums of southern California. A piece of rotating modern sculpture stood among thorny shrubs on the far side of the dim yard, completing if not balancing one's approach. Despite the good deal of money and attention it received, the area was used only as a shortcut to the science building, was home only to rusty bicycles, a chilly and deserted area attractive to no one so much as lost-looking pre-freshmen on tour of the college.

Regular students did not frequent the museum; occasionally they brought parents in on rainy weekends. But although he went there often to look through the print collection (which was quite good, if in the process of vegetable decay), James had never brought his mother there. Somehow the place kept him from it; he knew it would confirm any or all of her vague but strongly held suspicions about the whole of Modern Art. The grim building set between churchless steeple and space-age pinwheel was not where an aspiring artist brought his grimly skeptical mother. It did not impress. He took her to Smith instead, where afterward they could lunch in Northampton.

Ascending the hill, neither James nor Frank looked up toward the dark building but instead down at the steps, for they were discussing their work. All Gill had said weighed heavy on James' mind. He wondered if Frank would be capable of appropriate response.

"Do you feel cut off from all serious activities of life?"

"Not you *too*?"

"No . . . Gill was just saying that, though. . . . What can you say? Do you mind my asking?"

"Well, there are so many ways of looking at the situation. He does seem to know what he's talking about, doesn't he."

"He really does."

"Well, just because an intellectual dissociates himself from the world of commodities, from the brutality of bourgeois industry and from capitalist materialism as a whole—not that he's yet achieved that, by any means—and feels that as a result of this separation he can contradict bourgeois reality, or that he can deny the influence of the marketplace on the avant-garde, hardly gives him the right to tell a would-be artist that his work is insignificant, or that Art itself, because somehow tainted by capitalism, is insignificant, don't you think? I'm sure you do. Anyway, painting today may be insignificant to politicians, but it's not insignificant to artists. All aesthetic form contains anti-bourgeois qualities—responsibility, commitment, and real sensual realization in art, which combine to invoke revolution in the visual medium. He should probably encourage you, whatever kind of art you do and however trivial it is—if you understand me there."

"Yes," James said.

"Don't let him push you around. You know why?—Why?" The look in Frank's eye was very strange. "Why, then?"

"I give up."

"Because he's a cream puff," Frank said. "A cream puff. Don't forget that."

"No," James said cautiously. "I won't. Thanks."

"Don't thank *me*," Frank said, a broad grin spreading across his face. "Read Marcuse."

James shook his head up and down.

"Good man."

Gill and Joan met them near the abandoned steeple, where they had been trying its door. It was locked; Gill told them he had the key at home and might someday show them around.

"That's so like Gill," Joan said. "Connections everywhere."

They turned rather dutifully toward the museum, red-cheeked and wind-blown, stamping and shivering with the anticipation of warmth. The wind spun whirlpools of old dead leaves and dust in circles round the bleak courtyard; the pale, tomblike entry rose floodlit and the strange wind spun past. Standing on the threshold of their own strange and mysterious arrival, each happily calculated future satisfaction by the brisk discomforts of the physical present, but the warm glow of museum light alone could not account for their extraordinarily exhilarating anticipation. Higher above, the distant sky, briefly made visible through a rift in low dull clouds, held in its dark and glittering spaces the infinite abstract promises of summer and beyond.

Something was indeed about to happen, but not at Walpurgisnacht. There they would only find art. Joan left early and Gill and Frank disappeared after speaking briefly with Mrs. Merisi. James stayed late, if only because he felt an obligation.

A few weeks later school ended; Joan set off for the Greenfield Summer Festivale to act; Frank continued to plan his opening and tend his vegetables; Gill, oddly enough, disappeared completely to finish a number of incomplete papers, leaving James alone to begin his fellowship at his mother's apartment in the Bronx. Mrs. Merisi moved to her parents' home in the Boston suburbs, without selling any of her husband's paintings to Professor Pike. James wrote her several postcards that summer, to which for some reason she did not respond.

# PART II

# Mrs. Sloan
# at Home

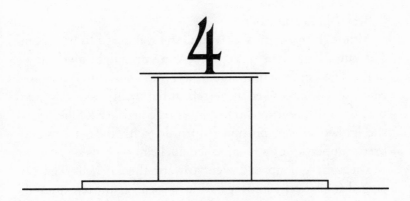

4

"Uh-oh. Look, Bean, it's Jamie."

Concern, apprehension, and resignation appeared as three vertical lines between Mrs. Sloan's eyebrows; her mouth tilted downward. Her face now resembled that of her son. He had said he would come some time this week; her intuition had done the rest. She could always guess the proximity of her offspring.

Bean, poised on the sill, gazed back with an aloof feline concern; Mrs. Sloan tapped his nose with her finger. He sniffed, chin up, inquiring, as Mrs. Sloan's expression reverted to its original: the unfocused eyes, pursed lips, and round satisfied cheeks of a cat. Only the slightest quiver of the head or the somewhat glazed eyes could possibly betray her to the casual observer, for something almost hysterical lurked below her placid exterior, permeating and saturating all aspects of her behavior, pushing through that iron-willed constitution like water through a dyke. She spoke incessantly to her cat and paced late into the night, alternately cleaning house and looking at herself in her several full-length mirrors.

"Better get decent."

Bean blinked in assent.

Although the night was warm, she wandered to her room and put a long, loose, deep blue robe over light blue baby-dolls. The combination suited her, she knew, in a quattrocento way. She looked at herself in her vanity, sideways, so that the reflection of a reflection presented her as she knew she looked best: a portrait in profile, with the set jaw and pretty upper lip of a renaissance duchess.

Then she got up and went toward the kitchen. The cat tagged at her heels, sniffing curiously, sensing the unexpected, meowing in expectation of what the unexpected would bring —Jarlsberg, or Ry-Krisp, or maybe lemon yoghurt.

But no, Mrs. Sloan would not have a snack. She did not want one and it was not what she usually did. She would not eat on Jamie's behalf. She was somewhat disturbed to be taken by surprise.

She walked to the living room and sat with careful posture on the edge of the sofa. Her routine had been spoiled by her son's unexpected arrival. She could not now go to bed as she would have liked.

Bean followed. She said to him, "It's just like him to do this to me. He doesn't know. If he did he'd probably do it anyway."

The cat stared long and hard.

"Of course not, no. But you must admit he's the most exasperating of the three. . . . He never listens. Always leaving wet towels on the furniture. Selfish, that's the word. And now he's an artist."

The cat meowed. She smiled again.

"Oh, is it food that you want?"

She shook her head, rose, went to the kitchen, and gave him a piece of Ry-Krisp. The cat stalked away from her to eat his cracker in peace. She followed him, not realizing that she did so; after watching him eat, she sighed, walked to the bathroom, and there took two more tablets from a prescription bottle from her psychiatrist. She looked at her face for a bit, sighed, then smiled and turned her head. Feeling much better, sort of floaty, she took her minted floss from the cabinet and wound a long green strand round one pale, manicured finger.

She was an assiduous flosser, always sure to floss after every meal; when her children neglected their flossing—she strongly suspected they did not floss much—she grew fretful, but in a way that made her feel good about her own habits of good dental hygiene. Besides, it settled her nerves.

The cat returned to sniff incuriously at her feet.

At length both resumed places at the window. Apprehensions and expectations now dulled, mother and pet drowsily contemplated the traffic once more, happily reconciled to the inevitable. Mrs. Sloan hadn't expected Jamie; soon he would be here, which was fine. Her formidable mind began to wander as she flossed, and staring out of her window, she thought of her children.

"They're absolutely perfect," she said, rewinding the floss on her thumbs. She used lots of floss, and was not ashamed of the luxury.

Bean nodded again, and blinked.

All three children had been delivered beside a highway, in a ward overlooking the East River, and grown up alongside several others: the West Side Drive, the Cross-Bronx Expressway, the Major Deegan.

"It's good for them, even if they were lonely. Character building, I think."

They had relocated every three years, traveling light through northern Manhattan and the Bronx, guided by the fantastic promises of the open road and the cardboard box.

"They're all very independent, you know; they know exactly what they want. They'll all be very successful."

James' two siblings had flung themselves resolutely and perhaps permanently from the Sloan nest in the past year. Katherine, the eldest, had left the Bronx for an easier life as a swamp-gas analyst in Louisiana, and had recently been meeting men. After dropping out of Penn State, Baby John had made enough money in computer leasing to buy a late-model Mercedes and a condominium in La Jolla, snapshots of which he had sent his mother at Christmas. Mrs. Sloan attributed these early successes to the complete independence she had granted her children at a tender age.

Just lately, she had moved with Bean to the Henry Hudson Parkway, Riverdale, the Bronx. The new apartment was perfect for one, but very small. It was the best neighborhood yet, almost the country, with a marvelous view of the highway.

"That's important. I'm very happy with it, though there's not much space. You like it, don't you? I do very much."

Bean scrutinized the carpet. As she continued to speak, Mrs. Sloan sensed her future hovering somewhere else, like the distant white glow of a late double-header at Yankee Stadium.

"And I'm certainly not about to take on a mortgage, not if every building in the country goes co-op, as they probably will. . . . Life's too short. If the economy holds up, things will get very nice for us, you know? Don't you think?"

The cat looked up again and blinked. He was used to this constant patter, and bore it well; much better, in fact, than any of Mrs. Sloan's children could. When Mrs. Sloan was in her pills the stream of recollection, justification, and misgiving was endless, and when the children were home, it got steamier, often ending in, or at least pausing for, tears.

"I don't care much for that suburban life, you know."

Floss made the ensuing words incomprehensible.

The highway outside was constant, reassuring, pleasantly noisy, as her family had once been. She turned to it now and fell silent.

The cat rose and stretched, then leapt from sill to coffee table, upsetting a geranium. Mrs. Sloan's reflexes were superb; she lunged, caught the pot, restored it, patted the plant, and as an afterthought plucked off a leaf that was yellowing but not dead. Even with pills, her mind was incredibly sharp and she was always ready for action. She loved action and argument; she was once a politician, now a lawyer, and would always be a mother. Catching plants was only one of a great many talents and abilities.

"I'm a devastating combination, you know."

Everything looked in order outside. She perked up, and went to look at herself in the mirror.

"Look how svelte, Bean," she said. "You might diet too. You're not what you used to be."

The cat lay curled on the sofa, quite still.

The drapy blue robe disguised sizable, well-toned biceps and a trim waistline. Mrs. Sloan recalled (with a smile) what Jamie had once said—that with her cool eyes, short curls, and set mouth, she reminded him of one of those busy occupants of the Sistine Ceiling, a sibyl in her niche who, perpetually reaching, turning, or jotting something down, is just a bit too composed in the presence of the infinite.

She bore his backhanded compliment with equanimity, sensing sibyls had always taken a lot of abuse and even so usually came out on top. As an attorney on the brink of success at midlife, ahead of the game even by her own rigorous standards, she was not intimidated by her son. She had toilet-trained him; he looked more like her than his father. Her sibyl-like composure would come in handy with him tonight. He needed a good talking-to and she was just the one to give it.

"What on earth is he up to, after all?" Looking about for response, she found the cat asleep.

Mrs. Sloan had not been awaiting James—only watching the traffic on the parkway—but she had, in fact, been thinking of him. That was her routine before bed: watch the traffic, check the plants, drink a glass of juice. Staring gave her time to think about things—pending litigation, personal finance, exercise class, and, always, of course, her children. With the possible exclusion of "Remington Steele" or "Cagney and Lacey," the window on the parkway was much more satis-fying than TV. Mrs. Sloan was not a recluse, exactly, but she rarely received guests in her home, preferring to do her so-cializing in the office. Not that her house was not presentable; simply, she chose not to present it. Now that Jamie—the artist—was coming, she had to collect herself.

She realized with a start that there were no clean sheets. That irritated her. If he couldn't call he'd have to live with it.

"He probably won't notice. Just like I've always said—he's in this world, but not of it. I don't suppose the artistic expect clean sheets."

She looked around her neat apartment.

"The point is, it reflects badly on me."

A truck passed noisily outside her window. With its passing the room became noticeably silent for the first time all eve-ning.

"Artist. I like the idea. The *idea* I have no problem with. But there's more to it than the idea—there's the day-to-day, the year-to-year . . . the *real life*."

She tried to picture her son as an artist: terminal syphilis, melancholic self-absorption, TV dinners, cutting off his ears.

"I don't care how worthwhile, Art will encourage all his worst habits. It's not the sort of thing I'd seen him doing; not what he wants. Imagine: dirty clothes, odd crowds, junk food. Not my Jamie. I know him."

She sighed and resolved not to worry. She knew she could talk him down, even if he was stubborn, even if she had not seen him for eight months.

The noise along the highway was sometimes deafening, then all but silent, and the crickets chirped and streetlamps buzzed alone until cars passed by ones and twos once more. James walked through waves of silence and noise, each equally palpable, savoring the late-night sensations of the parkway in June. Honeysuckle and primrose lingered among all the heavy green smells of summer and occasional patches of diesel exhaust. The stranger, floaty feelings of arrival and return, of city and country mixed, were no doubt enhanced by the dizzying fumes.

The scene was desolate after the crowds of Port Authority: a few silhouettes at windows; far ahead, a man walking a dog. James trudged on, his plastic bags bumping against bare legs, tired but happy, fully prepared for, even looking forward to, one of Mom's famous "talks." Around him, the soft, heavy foliage of early summer still held the day's steamy heat; deep, weedy grass by the roadside glowed silvery white; overhead the halogen lamps bent deferentially, casting on every surface their shimmery, greenish light, energy packed in thick wet air. The lamps buzzed, the cars pulsed by, the roadbed hummed in sympathy. He felt good being home, and strange: eager and desperate at once, as in the last moments of a distant swim under water.

Turning the matter over rather judiciously, Mrs. Sloan refused to feel sad.

"My children will never come back from college, only visit," she said, the statement hovering somewhere between declarative and imperative.

Her children would not come home. That was perfectly fine, certainly what must happen, and certainly what she would insist upon, if it ever came to that, as she suspected it might. There was life after motherhood; she knew and believed in it.

As the kids slipped from her thoughts, the surging procession of headlights upon the living room wall caught her distracted gaze, soothing and familiar, and with their smooth, quick passage more comforting than one might think. The apartment was, after all, too small for two to share comfortably.

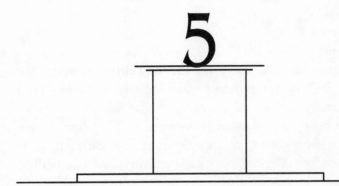

5

After turning on WQXR and a few more lights, she sat attentively on the edge of the sofa, head tilted to one side, listening for her son and stroking her cat.

"I suppose that's him in the elevator."

She rose and left the room.

Bean slipped cozily onto the nicest bit of sofa, where Mrs. Sloan had just been.

Distant footsteps, then a buzz, then Mrs. Sloan's bare feet; then a click and a scrape. Cries of excitement and surprise, bag-crinkling, and redoubled shoe-scuffs and foot-pats.

"How are you? You look great—"

"You didn't phone, dear. You should have. I might have been away or something. Did you lose your key?—not that I didn't expect that."

"Sorry."

James walked slowly into the room and flopped down on

the couch. Bean leapt from beneath him at the last possible moment and stood scowling on the arm of the sofa. James sighed, smiling; his mother, following close behind, stood over him, bending tensely to look at him.

"At least . . . any problems remembering which one?"

"No—"

"Tired?"

"Uh-uh . . . you?"

He knew she rose early for the long drive to work. She worked in New Jersey now; when she wrote him postcards she generally mentioned the exhausting commute.

"Not really. You look pale, sweetheart."

The eyebows were poised, the eyes beneath dilated; an expression relentless in its gently inquisitive way. Something was up.

"You're not sick?"

"I don't think so."

"All the art has made you tubercular."

He smiled.

"—though I'm happy for you, of course."

She folded her hands demonstratively, smiling a tight, nervous smile; the expression in her eyes did not change. "It must mean so much more than money. Much more than just money."

James shrugged and stared at the carpet, which was new.

She drifted back toward the window. "I'm not surprised —you remember all those things you used to bring home, the macaroni and yarn, the paper plates? Your teachers loved talking about you. How about some nice juice." She pattered into the kitchenette. "There's nothing in the fridge. I'm not running a restaurant. . . . I didn't even know you were coming. There's some yoghurt and Ry-Krisp, that's what I eat . . . not much, you know, not like the old days. . . . Just yoghurt—do you like lemon yoghurt?"

James and Bean stared at one another, unimpressed. Assorted openings and closings took place out of sight; the tinkle and clink of glass and ice followed in rapid succession; the small apartment fell silent but for the late-night sound of pouring fluids.

Mrs. Sloan reappeared bearing juice in stem glasses, handed one to her son, then walked to the loveseat across the room.

"You lose weight, Ma?"

"Oh, I don't think I'll ever get down to what I used to be."

"You look great."

Silence. Slurps.

"Aren't these glasses nice?"

"Yes. Thank you."

James followed up a considerable silence with another slurp, then took off his shoes and rubbed his feet.

He had seen the apartment only twice before. The furniture was new and just the sort of thing she'd always wanted. There was a matching sofa and love seat, two glass end tables, a coffee table, a wine rack, and small brass-bound chest. They looked very new and clean, especially in comparison to the stuff they'd had for so long. It was unquestionably her house. But then again, above him in the place of honor over the sofa was a large print he had done early his sophomore year. He had been proud of it then and made a great fuss about giving it to her that Christmas; now he disliked it intensely and she had had it framed.

He looked around once more. A few old familiar objects did survive after all: the tarnished bonbon dish, the bourbon bottle shaped like a wild turkey, the old brass spittoon in which she'd put a spider plant. Five years later it was still half-dead.

"So you've been doing well in art."

James nodded. "Dick—my professor—said I should apply to grad school. I might get an assistantship at RISD."

"That's something, isn't it?"

"Mmm-hmm."

"Is it your 'calling'?—I don't suppose that's the right word."

He stuck out his lower lip and drew his eyebrows together. "It's hard to say, Ma."

She nodded, and still feeling rather floaty, stuck out her lower lip and drew her eyebrows together.

He noticed a copy of *Self* magazine on the table before him. Its computer mailing label bore his mother's name. Looking up, he met his mother's apprehensive gaze.

"That artistic-consumptive look of yours is really too awful, dear."

"What's that?"

"Sure you feel all right?"

"We all look artistic around finals."

She nodded, and stared out the window. "Mmm. . . . You know, come to think of it, it's not very artistic looking on you . . . you're very handsome but there's nothing very *artistic* about you. Just a mother's opinion, of course."

James shrugged.

"You saw that article in the *Times*, didn't you? 'Hot Young Expressionists'?"

James sighed.

"You mean, 'The Hot New Abstract Expressionists.' "

"In the magazine. They had an artsy look."

"Mmm."

"I don't see you in that."

"They were European."

"You look it or you don't—or am I wrong?"

"Not neces—"

"Well, it's just a thought. You'd better work on it some. Just don't pierce your ears. That cat has never liked you."

Bean was stalking out, tail high, belly sagging.

"It might take longer than a summer to decide whether I want to do this as a career."

"Oh, someone will probably decide for you in any case."

Looking blankly at the print over his head, she added, "Of course, I'm no qualified judge."

James nodded.

"Mmmm. You know, loosening up, getting started, it may take an artist years. Even Franz Kline took years to get started. . . . He was only discovered eight years before his death."

"Who?"

"Franz Kline."

"Kline?"

"Yes."

She shrugged.

"You know Franz Kline. He does those really large black-and-white canvases—you know, 'rough impulsive gesture'?"

"*Did*, dear. He's dead. You just said so."

James clinked his ice. Bean returned from the kitchen and sat to scratch his chin. The room fell silent except for the sound of the highway outside, then the abrupt hum of the fridge turning on in the dim kitchenette.

"I like Hopper much better," Mrs. Sloan said. "I wrote a paper on him in school, you know. I went to the Met and they took the painting out of storage just for me. Of course, I had to write in advance for permission. It was a picture of a house next to railroad tracks . . ." she drifted off for a moment. Then, "While you're being artistic this summer you might also study for the LSAT's and the Foreign Service exam. This time off is a—"

59

"It's not time *off*. It's a fellowship."

She rolled her eyes.

"Yes, dear. This time that you have is a wonderful opportunity for establishing connections in business. Art is something the top-flight executives really like hearing about. I know that because I've seen it. They really do."

James stood up. She added, "We can talk about it in the morning, or whenever, dear. Right now I'm going to bed. I get up early, you know. I don't suppose you will."

She walked over to him, smiling, and, after he bent his head a little to allow her to do it, she rumpled his hair.

"What are your plans?"

"I thought I'd unpack, buy supplies, settle in . . . look into classes. You know . . . Why?"

"Surely you're not thinking of staying here?"

He looked at her, amazed; she looked straight back at him, or perhaps a little to his left and up.

"Of course, if you'll do the cooking and dishwashing and cleaning we might work something out, but I still don't like it. It's time you were out on your own . . . you must realize this place is . . ."

"I know. I'll start looking."

"Well, I'm hardly about to throw you out on the *street*, dear heart. You'll just have to keep very tidy and out of sight. That means no wet towels. And don't get too comfortable."

Walking toward the bedroom, she detoured to pick up his empty glass and brought it to the sink. "But you'll feel much better out on your own. That's a very hard thing for me to say, but now I've said it and I assure you I mean it."

James went to the linen closet and began rooting around for sheets. His mother came quickly to assist.

"You'll have to use a spread tonight, dear. I'm all out of

**60**

clean sheets. When I bought the new bed I cut down. . . . I didn't think I'd need them so I gave them to the thrift shop."

"My Road-Runner sheets?"

"Sorry."

"No . . . it's okay."

"And I didn't know you were coming tonight."

"I know."

"Sorry."

"I said, it's *okay*."

She smiled, looking tired. "You look much taller."

"You're skinnier. I haven't grown."

"I'm not as skinny as I used to be. I never will be, never like that, at least . . . I'm glad you're back. Good night."

They did not kiss, but instead patted one another on the arm. That night, with the cat keeping him company on the sofa, James sat up reading magazines until early morning.

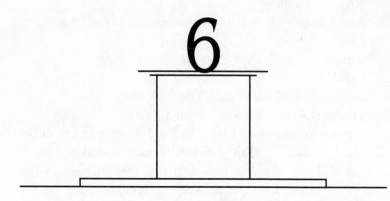

# 6

Mrs. Sloan woke earlier than James, and the first thing she did after her quick cold shower was to put on her high-heeled shoes and walk up and down past her son making loud noises on the parquet and blunt thuds on the hard carpet. One of the last things she did was feed the cat. While her hair dryer whined in the bedroom or the shower hissed in the bathroom, Bean leapt about the living room, particularly the sofa, pushing his wet nose or hot paws into James' cheek or groin or armpit, begging his daily nourishment. So as a rule James rose with his mother, made their coffee, and sat in the closet-sized dinette on a hard green stool, leaning against the wall and rubbing his eyes, all the time trying to block a growing awareness of his own physical existence.

While she warned her son extensively about the dangers of excess caffeine, Mrs. Sloan generally had a cup of his good coffee herself. She drank her coffee black from her one mauve

Wedgwood cup and saucer, and advised her son to drink his coffee black as well. He drank from a chipped imitation Meissen cup left in the back of the cupboard; happily so, for it was one of a set with which he had grown up.

"You can't possibly appreciate coffee with all the things you throw in it. You'd think we were at Chock Full O'Nuts," Mrs. Sloan would say in a tone that rarely varied. "Cream and sugar in coffee is ill-bred. . . . I won't try to stop you, of course, but I simply cannot understand."

And while she walked up and down drinking her coffee, holding the saucer chest-high and pacing from room to room, looking in the mirror lining the hallway between, checking her hair or makeup or standing sideways to observe the state of her waistline, she described the Nautilus center where she exercised, the new dress she had bought while in Paris on business, and her plans for travel in the coming year.

She did not plan to travel that summer. Her reasons were many: She did not want to or have to; she liked her office and the routine of going there each day; she had plenty of work to do; she liked her job as it was. Sometimes, though, she would stop in the middle of this discussion and gaze at him with the pursed lips, wide eyes, and slightly quivering eyebrows of chemically pacified motherhood. Then she would talk about a new sort of diet used in the treatment of hypertension or the latest type of skin care at Bonwit's.

After she left he would sit over his coffee another ten minutes, thinking how difficult a person she could be; then, à la Old Testament, start nervously into a morning routine of his own that paralleled in all ways the erratic and objectionable behavior of his mother. In these early days of his fellowship his energy was unbounded, and he bustled from room to room to do situps, shower, wash dishes, feed the cat, and make up the couch; then he would price art supplies and classes, research summer exhibitions, plan excursions to galleries, and call special numbers to find out about Art in Public Space; then he sat to figure his expenses in a black ledger bought specifically for the purpose. He would have to struggle to make his fellowship money last. He had no other money. Then he packed a lunch (peanut butter on raisin pumpernickel, a plum, a Tab), his supplies (eraser, journal, newsprint, charcoal, fixative, Nu-Pastel) and set out on the day's drawing, carrying his supplies in a small black rucksack. Then he would think what to buy for dinner that night, and how to cook it. He was not a good cook but he was learning.

Once he hit the street, though, a strange sensation of freedom and lack of a recognizable direction overcame him almost immediately. He had nothing to do but draw; no one to meet; no deadlines to shoot for and nothing, in short, to give his life any sort of coherence, form, or order. This free time, so agreeable to contemplate in the abstract, was a difficult thing to manage as it happened. Never before had he been so alone or so worried about something so unspecifiable; almost as soon as he left the house he began drawing as if his life depended on it, though it did not.

There was always the overwhelming question of where to go and what to draw. Generally he would walk over the Henry Hudson Bridge from the Bronx into upper Manhattan, simply because he liked walking over the bridge. Lifting him high over the landscape, far away from people and things, with only the wind, cars, and pigeons for company, it was nicest in early morning when the walkway was in shade and the air was still cool; then, if he were completely alone, he would leave pennies at intervals along the handrail to pick up, one by one, as the sun set on the way home. It was a safe game that he played rather often: few people passed over the bridge on foot, as a long walk through a dangerous park waited on the other side.

Some days, the best days, the sun rose bright and clear over the Bronx and Spuyten Duyvil. Ships and barges plowed up and down the river; the Circle Line passed at regular intervals under the bridge, full of tourists waving like celebrities to the one or two old men in straw hats fishing for eels and listening to AM radio. The Palisades sat grayish-brown and crusty on the Jersey horizon, uncanny in their resemblance to old pot roast. Whitecaps dotted the river; seagulls flecked the sky; at odd intervals bird and wave converged as sewers clanked open and birds sat afloat on cresting, refuse-strewn waves. It was a nice place to draw.

But mystery dissolves all too quickly into routine, especially as James' artistic impulse was of the type that languishes in direct sunlight. He found enthusiasm hard to sustain for hours on end, especially as there was no one else to talk to and nothing else to do.

The first weeks progressed smoothly. He kept himself busy drawing whatever he could, being careful to employ all the rules and guidelines of good pictorial composition. The days were so very much alike that even to him the whole experience, when he looked back on it, seemed to fade into a single all-day expedition beside the river and through the old neighborhoods. He drew old men on benches, kids playing at fire hydrants, ice cream trucks, bridges, warehouses, tunnels, and highways. Days of that sort, days of good weather and ambition and energy all around, were the best days of the fellowship. But there were other days as well, and as the weeks passed these other days tended to predominate.

Bad days began with minor catastrophes presaging ugly afternoons—Bean would vomit on the drawings, dishes would break, crucial supplies would run out. Sometimes he could think only of Marina, and how she must be doing real art, completely different and much more interesting, with people he didn't know; then he would think about Joan, and how she was learning and doing things that he would never be able to do. The worst days would begin in a brilliant and sweltering haze; the glare made his eyes tear, the smog made him choke. The bridge brought no relief; across the glistening brown expanse of river, the Palisades were a gray smudge on the flat white of the sky, and even at two hundred feet above the water the smells of human and industrial waste would waft up in dense, humid patches. On the other side he could see the rats hopping and scuttling among the rocks, and on every cool surface words like "Fuck" and "Cheryl" were scrawled in lurid aerosol paint. The air was close and stale, like a sickroom; the world coughed and gasped with the sounds of construction and diesel engines, and airplanes moaned like a Greek chorus as they circled on the LaGuardia landing pattern.

As he drew, drops of sweat fell from his forehead to his sketch pad, wrinkling and ruining his charcoal drawings; his head ached with the glare of the sun, and his eyes wanted only to close in the shade of some tree; his feet would blister and sweat in his worn-down sneakers, to which lumps of tar washed up by the river had stuck in nasty lumps. Days like that the world was very ugly, and he was no artist—with no one to talk to he had nothing to think about but that.

He would retreat back over the bridge some time after lunch, get home in midafternoon, turn on the air-conditioning, lock Bean in the bathroom, and lie on the sofa reading novels and eating hazelnut cookies. Not one of his friends had come to New York for the summer; his social life was nonexistent. The sofa was the best thing going. Often, feeling vaguely rebellious, he would neglect to use coasters, throw his socks on chairs, or leave wet towels on the bathroom floor. Then he would write a postcard or two to Joan and nod off during "Live at Five"; he was apt to be cranky when woken, and not good company. Mrs. Sloan would wake him with her arrival and talk to him a great deal. Often during this time in the afternoon their differences of opinion became pronounced.

One such afternoon a few weeks into the fellowship, the turning lock, ensuing scrape, and crescendoing click of shoes down the hall was only partially drowned out by the nearby slurp of sucked ice cubes and the turned-up sounds of "Live at Five"; James, absently watching Sue Simmons interview Grace Jones, resented the interruption, for the singer, clad in small strips of black leather, had been complaining in strident Caribbean intonations about customer maintenance at Crazy Eddie's appliance stores, and it was a problem he wanted to hear more about.

Mrs. Sloan said, "Hello, dear."

He turned toward his short, bright mother. She looked inquisitively at him but did not pause to speak, and soon running water announced her bath.

He rose and turned down the television. The room was silent except for the distant splashing of taps behind the bathroom door.

"Depressed, darling?"

Mrs. Sloan's voice, though muffled, was still insistently cheerful, the sort of voice one used while vigorously rasping a loofa over elbows and ankles. Leaning his forehead upon the door, James croaked, "Sort of."

His own voice seemed very far away, and he did not much care whether she heard. She knew he was depressed.

"Art's not very social, is it. . . . Did you do anything at all today? I don't suppose you met anyone interesting? Did you have a chance to buy groceries?"

"Yes."

"Good, dear. I wonder if Art makes one suicidal, or if the suicidal choose to become artists. Any thoughts? It's probably another phase. You go through more phases than your brother and sister combined. I suppose that's *exactly* what it is. I'm sorry I don't have much advice for you. I *do* know, however, that hard work will only make things better. Did you call Mr. Knowlton?"

Mr. Knowlton, president of a large public relations firm, had agreed to meet with Mrs. Sloan's son if he was seriously interested in the business.

"No."

By the stilling of taps and a quiet sloshing, James supposed his mother was relaxing, but with the passing seconds he found the absence of sound disquieting, an indication perhaps of disapproval. While he was comfortable with his mother's disapproval, he disliked its indication. She was very subtle with disapproval but he could sense it a mile off.

"You'd be good at lots of other, different things, Jamie. . . . I think you need a nice cozy environment. With a coffee machine, that sort of thing. Don't you think?"

"Eh."

"You were better at so many other things in high school. Before this Art . . . remember how good you were at chemistry, always on the phone working out problem sets? With your friend Ann? . . . I certainly do. And I remember you were much happier."

"I'm not bad at this."

"No, darling, of course not. But you shouldn't limit yourself."

The tone of her voice clearly indicated she had found him sprawled on the couch in midafternoon.

"See, Ma, you don't know what I'm doing. Why not see it my way for once?"

Sloshing water seemed now to indicate absorption in other affairs rather than downright disapproval. James began explaining his artistic concerns and preoccupations.

"That's sounds awfully complicated, darling. I can't imagine it's all they want you to do with your money. Perhaps you should show me some of your drawings."

"Mmm."

"I hope they're getting better."

He straightened. "Why do you say that?"

"No reason. Isn't that the point, though?"

He leant his head against the door once again.

Water sloshed.

"Hon?"

"Yes, Ma?"

"Would you start dinner, please?"

"Chicken okay?"

"Sure."

He went to the kitchen and put the broccoli in the steamer and the chicken in a baking dish and then into the oven. He was not very hungry on account of the cookies. After placing water in the steamer and the steamer on the stove, he returned to the door.

"How was *your* day?" he said brightly.

Silence.

"What, dear?"

"I said, 'How was your day?' "

"Fine. Is something the matter?"

"I was just wondering."

"Having work problems?"

**69**

"Sort of."

"You know, you haven't told me yet exactly what it is you're doing. Have you signed up for drawing classes yet? I think you need that sort of thing. Art school sounds much better than just wandering around on your own. You need a structured day, darling—an environment."

"My project is to do a set of finished drawings and prints of our old neighborhoods in Manhattan and the Bronx."

Silence. Then, "Why would you want to do that?"

"I don't know . . . I mean, I have several reasons, but I haven't really decided yet."

"My."

Sounds of massively displaced water put a temporary close to conversation. Over the throaty chuckle of the drain James began to talk some more about his work.

"It's not something *I'd* particularly enjoy doing," she said. "Why not take pictures? I think photojournalism is very exciting."

"No, that's not the point."

"Really? Well, I suppose you're the artist. *I* would take pictures."

The door opened, and Mrs. Sloan emerged, wet, bedraggled, her tired features brightly composed in an expression of great refreshment. She pecked him on the cheek. "How long will you—how long do you give it?"

"I don't know. . . . It depends what happens."

"That's nice. Excuse me, dear."

She walked into the bedroom, closing the door.

"How will we know if you're doing well? You don't seem to know that, do you."

Her voice was barely audible.

"I don't think I can," James said. "Not until my professors say something about it in the fall."

The house fell quiet.

"Here's what I'd do," Mrs. Sloan called through the door. "Write it down. Write down a schedule of all the things you want to do and all the things that actually happen. Then when you see how much you're actually getting done, you'll know you have to do more. Make a list. Set your priorities."

James looked back at the television set.

"Be as specific as possible . . . set your goals, try to achieve them, then either get them done in the allotted time and do more, or regroup and start again."

She started her hair dryer. She continued to speak, but was impossible to hear. James went into the kitchen and prodded the broccoli with a fork. Almost done.

When Mrs. Sloan emerged from her bedroom in her blue robe with her hair dry and fluffy, her son was again watching television; the broccoli was boiling over and the table was not set.

"Dinner's ready," she said.

They ate in the living room in silence, watching the news.

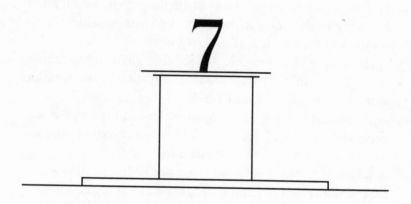

7

The Art Students' League on West Fifty-seventh Street had always intrigued James; he had known it by sight since childhood when, Christmas-shopping one cold, dry Saturday with his mother, he had noticed the building from a great distance and pulled her over to look at it. Since then, friends of his had always been about to take or thinking about taking or talking about a friend who had just taken some course there. A grandfather of art schools, promising bohemian fervor and nineteenth-century gentility, encouraging democratic art with a Whitmanesque flourish, pulling to its massive French renaissance bosom both amateur and professional alike, it was undoubtedly the best place for him to take a summer course. Classes were cheap, and the brochure promised air-conditioning.

The hour-long train ride from the Bronx had been constructive; he had drawn groupings and portraits on the A train, some of them shaky due to the rocking and slamming but interesting for the same reason. They weren't anything unless one knew they had been drawn on the subway. Which pretty well summed up his doubts about the project as a whole: too subjective, too dependent upon something not in the work itself. But soon he would be a real League member with a card to prove it, and *that* was something.

"After all," Mrs. Sloan had said, "you can't go walking around all *summer*."

Besides, part of the reason for being in New York was to meet real artists. He had chosen figure drawing, knowing that if there were any real artists at the League, he would find them in a figure class. He sensed that figure-drawing was like Zen archery, an activity of process rather than result serving to focus and refine individual energies, and therefore the sort of thing that appealed to every sort of talent. He was confident that interaction with other students would charge him with new ideas and challenge his older assumptions. The brochure had suggested that. And he knew from his experiences at Amherst that the stronger an artist's classical training, the less he could be faulted by his critics. Like spelling rules or multiplication tables, anatomy would always come in handy somewhere down the pike.

As he crossed the street, the ornate building rose before him, promising it was all an art school should be: big enough to be famous, old enough to be distinguished, French enough to be vaguely, artistically suspect in a neighborhood of glass, concrete, and steel.

The small flight of worn marble steps leading up to the main entrance served as a sort of grandstand for a crowd of people dressed in stained clothes and dark glasses, some staring in silent distraction while others chattered and waved their hands. All drank coffee from styrofoam cups. James approached behind a bearded midget in dark clothes and followed him up the steps through the absorbed yet watchful bodies.

The two sets of double doors led to a high-ceilinged, irregularly shaped lobby, most of its floor space taken up by an oversize bronze of a crouching youth, his patina disturbed by the sustained rubbing of hands and toes. The bench across from it held three securely settled-in shopping bag ladies, their belongings ranged carefully about them in small neat piles. One stared at him. The room was crowded; people constantly emerged from elevators, staircases, offices, and back corridors, but none stopped to chat.

He looked up. Paintings, mostly portraits and group portraits, but also still lifes, genre scenes, and a few dismal abstractions, occupied every inch of space beyond reach of the general public. Crusty, dusty, and dark, they were not yet so obscured by time as to disguise their off renderings or bizarre color schemes. But the overall grouping was effective in its way: in a strange combination of the baroque and byzantine, each heavily framed, cobweb-stranded canvas presented itself as a tile in a crazy mosaic describing, perhaps, the apotheosis of artistic mediocrity.

The registrar's office stood off to the right. He went in and met the midget once more, who pointed to the registrar's counter. "Lift me."

"What?"

"Lift."

James did so, but only after a moment of hesitation that seemed to offend the small man, who, when he had finished signing, plopped to the floor and stamped out, slamming the door behind him.

Turning to watch, James noticed a thin, wiry, red-haired

man in gold-rimmed spectacles behind him on line. The man smiled and shook his head. He looked very much like a rabbit.

"Happens a lot. It's just Henry."

"Oh."

"Registering?"

"Yes . . . figure drawing."

"I'm in that class."

"Do you like it?"

"I'm in it. You'll see."

"Walther Waeght?"

"The old Nazi himself."

As James did not know precisely how to take the last remark, he introduced himself. The red-haired man's name was George. James waited for him as he argued over the refund of a small sum, looking around the room with interest, for it was much larger than the lobby and densely packed with piles of paperwork on odd pieces of furniture. Small, well-worn paths had been cleared through the clutter. But more impressive than all this were the walls—or rather, the paintings that covered their every inch. Some of the works had come in the nicest of frames.

The arrangement here was quite different from that of the lobby. With the damp chill of the air-conditioning, the cavernously proportioned, dingily appointed room was more catacomb than chapel. The paintings, as a rule smaller and mostly indistinguishable in the half-light, were stacked to the ceiling not, one felt, in vain display so much as humble testimony to the institution that had overseen their creation. The collection evoked a way of life that, if not condusive to genius, was evidently thought worthwhile by many of lesser talent.

James had never before considered the existence of bad, thoughtful, well-intentioned art. This aspect of the trade, rarely represented in museum or textbook, produced a highly disquieting effect.

"Here for long?"

"Only the summer. You been here a while?"

"Six months. Got tired of selling real estate in Colorado, thought I'd come east. Always wanted to be an artist."

On the walk up to the studio James explained his fellowship and his subsequent decision to take a course.

"It seemed more legitimate than just doing whatever I wanted. I'm also sort of cut off from the art world up in the Bronx. And I wanted to see what real artists do."

George smiled. "It's all here," he said, "just like on TV."

They entered a high bare room on the third floor. Its little wooden chairs, raised platforms, paint stains, and clean-swept boards looked appropriately bohemian. The bells, hanging bulbs, and noisy clatter of students recalled movies about starving but talented inner-city youth. The effect—either so phony it looked real, or so real it looked phony—was in any case not unappealing. James felt right at home.

The students were another matter altogether. About half spoke of driving in from New Jersey or Long Island, and looked like housewives or bank tellers; the other half, which tended to cluster together in small chattering groups, looked rather too much like the real thing. One man wore overalls with no shirt; another sported a beret, pipe, and Chinese shoes; in the corner, a woman in a fashionably ripped white T-shirt spoke earnestly to another in peasant skirt, babushka, and black ribbed tank top. Many wore steel-rimmed glasses. Several carried bottles of Perrier water or small tubs of tortellini salad.

At an elevated desk in the corner, plainly staking out his position with baggage and art supplies, the tiny bearded man sat scowling. James noticed for the first time that he wore a monocle.

"What do you say?"

"Wow."

George patted him on the back and found a seat.

Two tired-looking people without supplies of any sort sat on the platforms. The one closest to James wore a grimy, patterned bathrobe; she had an enormous square medallion dangling freely from her equally large chest on a brown leather thong and was reading *The Dancing Wu-Li Masters*. As she read, her long slender fingers trailed through the still air from her mouth to a plastic bag of dried fruit and nuts. There the pale, hooked nails selected a piece, then raised it, slowly, carefully, to the waiting lips. The piece rested on the lips for a long moment, then the mouth opened, the tongue brushed the piece inward with a sideways motion, and the jaw moved deliberately. The lips stirred slightly and then came to rest. The throat undulated. The process began again with a new, different piece.

George leaned over and said, "Gloria," adding with a gesture, "va-voom."

James observed that, rather in spite of her distinguishing feature, Gloria bore a marked resemblance to his paternal grandmother.

"Where's Walther Waeght?"

"Didn't they—? No . . . He's only in on Tuesday and Thursday."

A bell rang and a monitor appeared, youngish and emaciated, redheaded like George. He called the poses. The class came to order. All talking ceased.

Gloria was indeed disproportionately well-endowed, yet for this reason, and perhaps also because she refused to remove her medallion, no drawing James did of her looked quite right. He managed a few comprehensible likenesses that did not seem to make sense; the fault was in the body, not the observation. Looking about, he noticed that most people did not even attempt to draw the models as they appeared, but instead created figures of exaggerated musculature arranged in similar poses, the general style tending to recall either Pietro da Cortona or Marvel Comics. Many people added rocks and swirling drapery for effect.

At the long break everyone walked downstairs and sat on the steps to drink coffee and gossip. James stared at the people going by while George spoke animatedly about his drawings and puffed upon a cigarette. The midget sat behind them speaking in low tones to a red-haired woman in bloomers.

". . . Pretty nice drawings," George concluded, tapping out an ash.

"You too . . . Tell me, does everyone in the class draw in a particular way, or is it my imagination?"

George considered the remark, nodding slowly.

"Certainly . . . Waeght won't have it any other way. You'll hear from him soon enough. He won't like you much. . . . your work's way too tame. Not enough meat."

"Oh."

They watched the traffic.

"George, are you a professional artist?"

"More or less."

"What do you do?"

"What do you mean?"

"What sort of things do you make?"

"Well, I draw."

"Are you a printmaker?"

"No, never tried that. I do drawings."

"What kind?"

"I draw nudes."

"Really?"

"Though I haven't sold any yet."

"No?"

"I'm not really good enough yet."

James nodded. "When do you think you'll start?"

The bell rang at that moment, and George shrugged, leaving the question unanswered. Later that evening, when his mother asked him a similar question, he remembered the blank, odd look in George's eye and wished he hadn't asked.

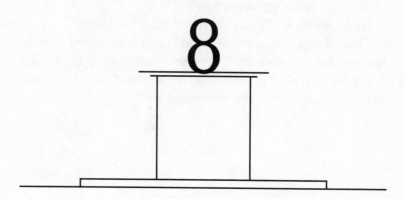

8

"He's doing it to spite me," Mrs. Sloan said. "The problem is, it's working."

She was sitting on the edge of her bed, holding a hairbrush, talking to the cat. Being kept home from work with a cold would mean missing not only an important meeting in the law department, but her aerobics class as well, and as a result she was more than generally on edge. With her routine disrupted and her environment changed, she had been in her bathrobe all day.

"I did Art once, too, you know," she had been saying to the cat. "I'm not the philistine he makes me out to be. I won a summer scholarship just like his in high school, to the University of Chicago. . . . I haven't saved any of the artwork, of course, we've moved so often. I think my mother may have some of it—not that it was worth saving or anything."

She looked at herself in the mirror on her dresser, feeling

terribly frumpy in her robe and in her home, vulnerable to all sorts of personal recrimination. It wasn't like her office, where she was boss. That was a stable environment. The apartment was less safe; she knew Jamie resented not having a place to sleep, felt it in his every gesture.

"I expect he holds that against me. Well, I don't really feel compelled to apologize. I'm sorry that I don't know enough about Art to hold my own in a conversation with him, but I've told him I don't find it the most riveting subject. And I'll tell you another thing," Mrs. Sloan added, looking directly at the cat, nodding her head sagely. "*He* doesn't find it a very riveting subject. He doesn't like it like chemistry. He *liked* chemistry. He did chemistry all the time."

The cat ran out of the room. Soon after, feeling slightly thirsty, she rose and went to the kitchen, filled a saucepan with water and set it to boil, then dropped a low-sodium French bouillon cube in the water and watched it dissolve. When nothing happened she broke it up with a spoon.

She had been increasingly worried about her son in the past few weeks. He had no girlfriends, did nothing at night except touch up drawings. He seemed so aloof, so disconnected from the real world. It wasn't healthy. She had talked to her psychiatrist about him; like all good psychiatrists, he had reaffirmed her in her doubts. She knew Jamie had changed at college, a college she had not wanted him to attend. Just as obviously, he had taken up Art because he was unhappy.

She adjusted the pan on the flame. The water fizzed and hissed. The air conditioner was on. It was a hot, ugly day out, not the kind of day *she'd* want to be traipsing around New York in, artist or no.

"And what the hell kind of art is it, anyway?" She suddenly asked aloud. "He'll never make it with that sort of thing."

Although she had long since given up all prospects of a

wealthy son, she couldn't bear to think he should waste his time so strangely. Even *she,* a lawyer who worked at a mall in suburban New Jersey, knew that modern fine art was a patently bogus business designed to help rich people save money on taxes. Jazz and movies were the real art of America and they didn't go asking for handouts from anybody. It was all very nice to say your son was a printmaker, but to see it happen in real life was nothing but sad.

"Well." She poured the bouillon into a mug and went to the living room, sitting by the air-conditioner to drink it.

"Bean, no . . . no. Well, all right." The cat settled into her lap, warm and shedding.

He meant so much to her. Sometimes in the past week she had found herself, in the middle of work at her office, staring out at the parking lot and the mall across the street, thinking what her son could be up to.

She honestly had no idea.

"No, no, no. That's not right, honey. You'll never be an artist if you draw like that. That must be the worst drawing I've ever seen in my life."

James was sitting at the League in the lobby with the shopping bag ladies. One of them, surrounded by bags and pieces of plastic, had seemed like a good subject for a drawing, and with a half-hour free before class he had set to with gusto. Now he had finished and shown it to her and was paying the price for artistic indiscretion. But as almost all the great artists of the last century had suffered so much more for so much less, and the statements of bag ladies counted for so little in the critical world, he could only smile and chalk up one more victory for the Art Students' League. After several weeks, though he still had reservations, he was enjoying himself immensely.

Henry the midget had turned out to be an extraordinarily good if mannered draughtsman; James liked standing with him over breaks and looking at his drawings. He didn't say much, but so far James had learned he was a graphic artist who did cartoons and posters for the performing arts when he could and took serious classes at night. For the summer he had decided to do anatomy as a break from his serious studies. While James respected his ability and persistence, he liked him mostly because he was the only other person in Walther Waeght's class who did not draw like the old man himself.

Mr. Waeght, a crotchety septuagenarian with a Van Eyck face, barely managed to come in once a week, which was, though a surprise, hardly a distressing one. James drew well enough without supervision; when Waeght did come in it was to scold James and Henry repeatedly for not drawing the poised heroic musculature locally attributed to Third Reich Art. Other members of the class looked upon the two of them as hopeless, especially just after Mr. Waeght had given a demonstration, for he was very good at what he did. So as a rule James and Henry kept to themselves, toward the back far side of the room where no one except George would come near.

The regulars had resolved into several opposing, somewhat interesting groups. The older artists sat in the best corner, close to the door and the air-conditioner. They drew just like Mr. Waeght, and measured all drawing by its resemblance to their teacher's. Most appeared to have been in the class for a very long time and walked around in groups of two or three on breaks speaking with condescension of other people's drawings. In the corner opposite sat a group of young, fashionably artistic women whose work, if not exceptional, did show more independence of spirit. Two had just quit publishing to write and illustrate children's books together.

Then there was a sizable contingent of those who could

not draw at all, and beside them the odds and ends: James, Henry, a few occasional others.

The day had begun well, if hot and humid. He had drawn light effects on benches and alleyways near Morningside Park and done a number of life drawings in a good cheap coffee shop near the Cathedral of St. John the Divine; now he was perfectly content to sit in the air-conditioned studio for a few hours of uninterrupted concentration, the most restful sort of hard work.

Gloria's new poses, standing and bent double, or, alternately, on her back with her legs in the air, required tricky manipulations of perspective. James did well at this. By not drawing the medallion and reducing the breasts to comprehensible proportions, he also managed one or two good-looking drawings. He was trying as well to frame the nude he was drawing compositionally—to arrange the figure in space so that the drawing, when it was completed, was interesting not only for its rendition of the figure, but also for its massing of light and dark, and its counterpositionings of textured and solid surfaces over the picture plane. Lately, not content with the model alone, he had taken to drawing the entire class at work, with some startlingly good fast portraits.

Gloria was still his favorite model, for her body was the least oddly shaped. The models seemed in general to have been selected for their impossible musculature; one especially strange man had a body so overbuilt that his neck had disappeared into one big wedge between his shoulders, and his limbs stood out from his torso like a bulldog's. Unlike his, her poses varied nicely; unabashed by her own flexibility, she did a good *Conversion of the Magdalen* and a devilish *Christina's World* (though she did wobble or grow limp with poses that required standing, like a *Birth of Venus*, say, or—James' favorite—*The Awakening Conscience*).

The bell rang and poses were called for a little more than an hour. When break was called, James went next door alone to the Gristedes to buy his coffee in a styrofoam cup. He went back and sat on the steps feeling very much like an artist, just like the ones he'd seen the very first day of classes.

A group of break dancers occupied the space just beyond the awning, separated from artists on the steps only by the tide of pedestrian traffic sweeping toward Seventh Avenue. They were spinning on their heads to barely audible music, apparently with hope of making money. Rather than watch them he went back upstairs.

George was looking at his drawings. "Interesting."

"I liked your last one a lot."

"We've both got long way to go, though."

"I guess."

The final pose of the day was called. Gloria sat backward on a chair.

"One hour," the emaciated monitor called.

The room fell silent but for the smooth scratching of Nu-Pastel and charcoal on newsprint, the deep-drawn breaths of concentration and absorption. There was the occasional rustle of sheets of paper, and subdued clearing of throats. James thought, while drawing, how little any of this compared to the drawing sessions he had had in Dick Merisi's class, but then again how much more pleasant it was.

Gloria yawned.

James thought once again of Marina, wondering where she was and what sort of art she was doing.

Henry drew with his eyes narrowed, bent down over the page, his hand moving rapidly and body shaking, like a cat dreaming. Gloria watched him; James watched her.

After a while he stepped back to look at his drawing. It was not as good as the earlier ones; he had spent too much time working and reworking the image, so that it had a flat, smudged quality, lacking the sense of moment, the insistent, drawinglike quality of his best. With ten minutes left he closed up his pad to leave.

He returned home to find his mother deeply engrossed in "Live at Five," emery board in hand, repairing a broken nail with a kit. An empty spool of dental floss sat before her on the table and a wastebasket at her feet. The blast of the air-conditioner had necessitated raising the volume of the television, so that from the time he entered until he turned both down they could not speak. He knew that, apart from her cold, something was bothering her (she had looked restless and worried for weeks), but he also knew that if she wished to share her problems she would do so at her own convenience.

"Hello, dear. How was your day?"

She sawed virtuosically upon her index finger as she spoke, her whole body shaking with the effort.

"Well?" she said brightly.

"Okay . . . you?"

"What's that, dear?"

"You feeling okay?"

"Yes. Fine. Much better. You know, it's about time I saw some of your work."

"Thirsty?"

"Mmm."

James went to the kitchen and poured two Tabs into the new stem glasses and added ice. In one of them he put lime. He didn't usually bother with ice or glasses but today it was necessary; his mother liked Tab in glasses with ice and lime, especially since she had bought new glasses. He returned and they sat and drank together, son on sofa, mother on love seat. After a minute Mrs. Sloan rose and turned down the television.

"Thank you, dear, you're wonderful to remember the lime and the ice. I know you don't generally do that for yourself. I appreciate the thought. Were there any breakthroughs today?"

James raised his eyebrows. "Not really," he said after a thorough consideration of the question. "I think that as long as I work hard I'll be fine. . . ." He trailed off, and looked at her for a moment with a concerned, puzzled expression.

"Hard work *should* pay."

He shrugged. "Still want to see those drawings?"

"Certainly."

"Okay, then."

James fetched the newsprint and a few of the better finished drawings, turned off the television, and spent some minutes explaining his aims and methods. Mrs. Sloan peered at the work over her reading glasses, lips pursed, filing away.

He concluded. She nodded attentively. He put the drawings back. She said nothing. When he returned, she seemed to be thinking of something else entirely, with her nose slightly wrinkled and her eyes narrowed almost to nothing.

"Isn't there something humorless about this business?" She finally asked. "The Art business, Capital A, *Art?* I never see really absorbing art anymore. Maybe artists are actually threatened by that kind of approachability. I'm sure they aren't as good as they used to be. Maybe I'm perfectly wrong. I suppose I am. . . . I don't mean *your* art, of course, just art in general. But really, darling, nobody really *enjoys* modern museums. They're very swank, and if you're visiting New York you go there after you've been to Saks—it *is* right up the street from Saks, you know—you can go there in new clothes you've just bought, or take a date, but you know what I mean."

"I don't think I do," James said. "I think that with education the most difficult things begin to make sense."

"That's just like you. But remember the last time we went to a museum? Two Christmases back, for the Hopper exhibit? We sat in the little coffee place drinking *caffè latte* almost as long as we walked through the show."

"That show really wore me out, Ma. We needed that coffee to *recuperate*. Hopper is an enormously powerful artist."

"As I remember you did the crossword."

They sat silent as Mrs. Sloan smiled at her son and sawed on her nail. James played with the dental floss container.

"Have you read this?" She held up a paperback biography.

"No."

"Don't, darling. Or maybe you should."

"Why?"

"I bought it in softcover for my last trip to Europe. I was looking through it today. It's all about drugs and sex and violence and the art business. I don't know if it's accurate, of course—how should I? I'm no artist. But it *was* listed as nonfiction in the *Times*. And it's awful. Really horrid. A quick read, if you want to poke through—been a best-seller for ages."

"Is that what you're upset about? I hear there's a lot of sleaziness in the art world—"

"That's it. Sleaziness."

Mrs. Sloan's eyes focused momentarily on her son, with a look at once knowing and uncertain.

"It's hardly why I wanted the fellowship."

"I admit that it's very *absorbing*. I admit that freely. Of course I do. It's an interesting book."

He shrugged.

"Well, none of those artists seemed very happy. In fact, most of them died. It may have only happened in the book, but it's true. They were the ones making money, darling—the ones who had made it."

She broke off again.

James went in to get another Tab, taking his mother's glass as well.

"No more for me, thanks. Did you know that the first thing that Andy Warhol did when he started making money was set up an apartment for himself and his mother? They lived together in a tiny little place . . . look. Here's a picture of it."

"No kidding."

"Yes. So tell me," she said, raising her voice so he would hear as he ran water into the sink. "Are you trying to insinuate yourself into contemporary avant-garde decadence? Is that why you want to be an artist?"

James returned with the Tabs.

"Nobody's thrilled with their work all the time, Mom." He sat down. "I mean, I worry all the time, but that's how it's supposed to be."

"Why are you doing it? Really. Please tell me honestly and I won't trouble you anymore."

"Really?"

"Really."

He looked at his mother, and for a moment he was the child she had once known, with wide, distant eyes, slightly scared.

"Well, I can't sit home all day, can I? It beats working at Burger King."

"You could do a lot of other things."

"This is what I'm doing now."

She sighed. "No avant-garde?"

"Your guess about the avant-garde is as good as mine. I find out about it from reading *Vogue*."

"They sound like awful people."

"C'mon, Ma. The avant-garde is *supposed* to disturb people

like you. Their whole function is to transgress bourgeois values, implement change through shock."

Mrs. Sloan put down her file. "What do you mean, 'people like me'?"

"My friend Gill knows more about it than I do."

Mrs. Sloan's expression drifted from indignation to worry. "That reminds me," she said. "A friend of yours called. I think his name was Gill."

James sat up. "Really?"

"Mmm-hmm. But to get back to what you were saying. No avant-garde interests?"

"I don't know. Not unless I run into Marina. What did he say?"

"Marina?" Mrs. Sloan said, eyes brightening. "What's Marina up to?"

He sighed. "I wrote her this semester and she wrote back—she's an artist now."

"Well, that's something. She's that wonderful girl with the definite look of success . . . do you have her number? Have you called her yet?"

"I'm working on it. But what about Gill?"

"Do, Jamie. She'd do you good. She was always so interesting. Some people just have a spark about them, you know, some sort of quality that sets them off—Here. Use a coaster—she was very beautiful. Rich, too."

James wiped the spot from the glass tabletop and set his drink upon a coaster that matched both sofa and carpet, and looked rather warily at his mother.

"Her father is."

"She's really avant-garde?"

He shrugged. She picked up her bottle of nail glue.

"Can art really make you happy, dear?"

"I don't know. Sometimes." He knelt on the floor to play

with the cat, scratching its belly and waving his hand over its head. "I mean, that's kind of an unfair question," he continued. "It's like anything. I think it's satisfying in the long run. Like anything."

"Hmm."

"Anyway, I like doing it for now."

"If you say so, dear. You just look so put-upon."

"You don't look so chipper yourself."

Mrs. Sloan considered for a moment. "I make truckloads of money."

They laughed.

Mrs. Sloan looked down, applying glue to a nail, and grew oddly serious. "You take such an optimistic view. You'll never put your children through college. If you have them."

He looked around the tiny apartment at its simple new furnishings. "Nothing wrong with optimism."

Mrs. Sloan, concentrating on a tricky bit, did not look up, but began slowly to nod. She seemed to be thinking. The room fell silent until the nail-mending was done.

"I realize it's more for you than earning money. I respect that. But don't forget how important money is, how little anything else matters when you're starving. We had it rough once. I don't want that to happen. I won't be around forever."

"I don't want to fail because I'm afraid of being hungry."

"That's not failure, dear. That's real life. Now would you start dinner?"

"Sure."

"I'd like a nice chop and some vegetables, steamed lightly with fresh dill."

"Green beans?"

She nodded. As he puttered around the kitchen she said, "You know, dear, I worry about you all the time. You'll excuse me, as I'm your mother and entitled to say this. You're

**91**

awfully withdrawn and this art makes you worse. Don't you want to enjoy yourself, have a little fun?"

"It's my life."

"What?"

"I said, 'It's my life.' "

"What's that supposed to mean? I asked you if you wanted to enjoy yourself."

"It's my life to enjoy."

"Of course, dear."

"Well."

"I think you should."

Silence; the clanking of pots and sound of running water.

"You know, you're right. I *have* been having fun, in a depressing sort of way. But it's really not enough."

"What?"

"Something has to change."

"Really, dear? Good. I think so, too."

But her voice was less than decisive. She fell silent after that and James did not volunteer more information. He did not know if it would still be possible to go live at Gill's but he would find out. Right now things did need to be more fun, but perhaps more to the point, though he loved his mother, he had to get out of her apartment.

After dinner that night Mrs. Sloan helped with the dishes, and afterward, for the first time in years, they played a desultory game of Scrabble that ended in a draw when Bean upset the board.

# PART III

# Happy
# Artists

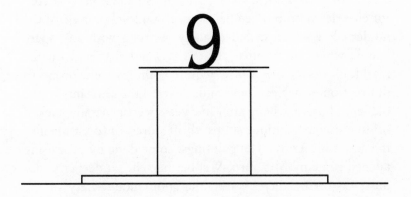

Too impressive and too full of belongings to impress one
immediately as a home, the Brix-Webber apartment was a
cluttered and confusing place where, for years, the eclectic
taste of Gill's mother, a collector of wide interests and great
enthusiasm, had run rampant to the delight and dismay of
family members and their invited guests. Objects of ungainly
and grotesque loveliness crowded the spacious rooms: mar-
ble-topped tables of dubious origin standing cheek-by-jowl
with Queen Anne china cabinets; Victorian daybeds nudging
complacently against Shaker sewing cabinets, Regency otto-
mans holding their own against the blue satin banquettes of
a folded Venetian brothel. On every available surface was a
collection of some sort of another: Eskimo carvings in soap-
stone, pewter salt cellars, blue Nankin china, Art Deco cocktail shakers, Chinese cricket cages, Balinese fetishes, sculpted
crystal pigs, and museum reproductions of the King Tut bust.

Gill had become an avid collector while still in grade school, and his reclusive father had often returned from his international financial dealings with boxes and crates in tow for both wife and son. While acquisitive, the family was never very careful of its treasures; their chandeliers had all been altered for electricity, amputated below a certain level because of the modern low ceilings, and casually restrung with any spare bauble when the original crystals fell and shattered on the marble floors below. Once acquired, things were prone to destruction or neglect; new finds covered the remnants of the old, and those surviving after five years were generally packed off to museums, antique shops, thrift stores, or (occasionally) the Salvation Army. The paintings, some done by promising talents, some by Mrs. Brix-Webber herself, sat deeper under dust, dissolving thereby into the anonymous safety of the paneled walls on which they were hung. None had been touched, and few looked at, in the past ten years.

The Brix-Webbers had been suing their landlord for about as long. Despite its great expense and magnificent location the place bore the unmistakable signs of modern apartment life: the rooms were stuffy and dark, with paneless windows of ignoble proportion set at inconvenient intervals (except in the master bedroom, where Mrs. Brix-Webber had inspired the landlord's countersuit: now a large bank of windows faced out onto the park). The ceiling was falling in throughout the house; patchy and rust stained, it dropped great loads of textured plaster substitute at irregular weekly intervals, usually by night. The house therefore stood in perpetual disarray, with water stains and plaster piles holding their own against paintings, furniture, and china, ready to impress insurance claims adjusters who might, for all anyone knew, arrive at any moment. Lately another disruption, the arrival of Gill's possessions, had brought new piles of things to a thing-piled place. Books and cameras and art objects of a collegiate sort stood with clothes and tennis rackets in unmanageable heaps in the study, guest room, and Gill's own bedroom. Mrs. Brix-Webber had herself left just that afternoon to join her husband in Antibes, and her bedroom and study (where many of her summer clothes were kept in the drawers of a Louis XIV escritoire) still bore the signs of frenzied and hysterical packing.

James, who had been out drawing all day, sensed that though the house was large enough to accommodate everyone, he had unwittingly brought trouble and strain. Dolly had a cold and could barely manage the housekeeping; Peanut, the ill-tempered shar-pei, had apparently chosen to express grief for his departed mistress with a vehement case of diarrhea; and in the past week family members, each arriving and departing with the glorious fanfare of a Cunard Liner, kept the place wild with confetti and champagne, and had made James' stay even more unrestful than he had thought possible in any apartment outside his mother's small one-bedroom uptown. Still, he was thankful for room to stow his four plastic bags and two cardboard portfolios; moreover his financial situation had stabilized at $675.29.

He sighed and rolled over on Mrs. Brix-Webber's vast bed, which smelled lightly of perfume, medicine, and real linen sheets. The sun had set late over the Central Park West sky-line; between writing journal entries and touching up a draw-ing of the Highbridge Aqueduct, he had spent one afternoon drinking coffee and talking to Dolly. Now it was dark and she was asleep in her room. Gill was out for the evening and Mrs. Brix-Webber had left the country.

Scattered objects in the opulent room stirred slightly with the cool breeze off the park; the long, gauzy curtains swayed backward from a wall of glass revealing the sunset; here the dust ruffles on the chaise, there the unopened mail, piles and piles of it, quivered slightly and then fell still. A warmish night, but at this elevation and with this view, cool and pleasant. Mrs. Brix-Webber's bedroom was a good, safe, comfortable place to be, but even so James was not yet fully at ease.

For this reason, after writing a lengthy and considered journal entry he picked up the ivory princess phone and, consulting his worn address book, began to dial a long sequence of numbers. After six rings, several inquiries, and repeated fumblings, a sleepy and disconcerted voice answered. Joan had been napping on her day off.

"Hi. It's me."

"Who?"

"Me. James."

"Scooter?"

He had called to discuss careers, ostensibly hers. While neither the brusque, unrelenting immediacy of phone conversations long-distance nor their price had much appeal for him, he missed her terribly and, more to the point, needed some advice. To date, she had answered his three letters with a postcard of the hairpin turn on Route 2 in North Addams. Luckily, since he had woken her up, a few halting sentences of theater gossip rapidly gave way to the topic of his choice.

"Enough about *Damn Yankees*. How is it?"

"Glad you asked."

"She's giving you a hard time. . . . I knew it."

Joan, as the result of a brief but memorable exposure to the Brix-Webber apartment the previous year, had come away with a store of misinformation that had given a distinctly Gothic flavor to James' own first moments in residence. She recalled the house as a tiny, twelfth-floor Versailles, presided over by Gill's mother, an impossibly neurotic and typically French chatelaine-cum-homemaker.

"No, she's very nice actually, and she left yesterday. But to tell the truth, I really don't know *what* to think about Gill. He keeps talking about this social commitment and art stuff." He broke off. "It's weird talking Art for the Masses in this place."

"Ridiculous."

"And I feel so *kept*. It's a nice change but it's no way to live."

"Just promise yourself you'll do for someone what he's doing for you. Don't make problems for yourself, Scooter. It's boring."

"I don't *want* to. But—take last night. I come home late and Mrs. Brix-Webber stops her packing to make sure I eat dinner. She gets Dolly out of bed. Dolly throws out the first dinner she's cooked for me and makes another. *Fresh*, she says."

"Really?"

"Mmm-hmm. Steaks."

"Steak?"

"Steaks, plural. With asparagus, watercress salad, a '74 Pomerol and a napoleon from Dumas—the whole shebang. Do you know they buy groceries from the Gristedes across from the Whitney Museum? Dolly just told me that today."

"Holy cow."

"So, afterward, I'm talking to Dolly, who looks really worn out. She starts telling me she's Hindu—"

"So?"

"—and that the *idea* of beef gets her violently ill. Which, I had to assume, was why Mrs. Brix-Webber had to get her out of bed. And there she is, pan-frying my steaks every night for as long as I stay. I tried to have chicken but the chicken is for the dog. It's all been planned out."

Silence. "You realize, James, that I haven't had a steak since the Junior Class Dinner?"

"That was bad steak. This was the kind they fly in from Wyoming in a box."

"No."

"Yes. And—"

"What now?"

"Homemade butter curls."

"No."

"Yes."

"And you want my sympathy?"

"Joan, please try to understand."

"Hold on. I'll try."

James heard the clunk of a receiver on a hard surface, then silence. Then, "Okay, what's the problem?"

"Where'd you go?"

"I was screaming."

"Oh." Silence. "Sorry."

"It's okay."

"Well, my problem is how to deal with Gill. And how to make sense of all this."

"He's no dummy, Scooter."

"He seems to expect something from me."

"I wouldn't say too much, either. It would only get you in trouble."

"The thing is, he's so *charming*. He's chic and connected and he's got this very high I.Q. and manners that are straight out of a funeral home. If he's not talking Marxist aesthetics he's staring at me through his glasses with these big wide bluefish eyes. He's so . . . *intense*."

"He can be intense if he wants to. It's his house."

"I know. And I think he knows I think he's intense, and I also think he takes it kind of personally."

"How."

"He's much more moody than at school . . . I don't think he's having a very good summer. He works at a soup kitchen and I think he's also trying to write something. He doesn't talk about it but I hear him typing."

"You know," said Joan, the tone of her voice suddenly different, "he must be really insecure."

They laughed. Insecurity was their private catchall, a word that had, for as long as either could remember, condoned if not excused every type of ridiculous behavior, from excessive face washing to joining fraternities.

"No, really, Scooter. You're helping him out. He wants to help people. It's his thing."

"I don't like it."

"Nobody asked you."

He tugged on the phone cord, wondering whether letting her give all the advice was good for the politics of their own relationship.

"You've got a point."

"Not to change the subject, but what's he really like?"

He knew she had sensed his hesitation and accordingly modulated her voice from its former terse monotone of dutiful concern to something new, less soothing, and much more real: a conspiratorial whisper of piqued curiosity. She had always wanted the dirt on Gill.

"Okay," he said, lying back and smiling. "Well, when he wants something from you, you really know about it. He keeps asking me these intensely theoretical questions about art."

"You said that already."

He sighed.

"You want to hear, or not?"

"Okay."

"Well, I get the impression he doesn't know what to do with himself lately. None of the People Worth Knowing came back here from school, and his New York friends are all out of town too. He wanders around a lot, buys a lot of things, books especially. . . . He's got shelves and shelves of them, and I've noticed . . ."

"What?"

"None of the bindings are cracked."

"Wow."

"And he collects lots of little antiques, too—his mom told me he's been collecting Spode since he was six. Nowadays it's mostly contemporary paintings, which from what I can tell he acquires for a gallery. At least, none of it comes here. There's no room for it. Of course he doesn't talk about his own collecting with me. He's very modest."

"Mmm."

"No career plans, at least he never talks about it. But you know, every day I spend with him I'm more sure he's going to be a phenomenal success in business someday. He's like a little kid in a lot of ways, but just below the surface I sense this . . . well, hard to describe exactly . . . I guess you could call it a *capitalist killer instinct*."

"Wow . . . neat. I'd never have guessed."

"Of course, he still finds time to teach me Central American politics in his spare time. He's very Politically Correct."

"Does he talk about theater at all?"

"Not with me. But he's been staying in a lot, like I said. I saw *Richard III* in the park, though. The sword fight was amazing."

"I know, I know, I read the review. I just thought he might have a scoop on something really *in*-teresting."

"Mmm." He opened his journal and began to doodle. "So."

"Well, I'm pretty jealous of you. Think of me. Macaroni and cheese in Greenfield."

"We should switch."

"We should."

"You know, I might leave here soon to do work-study at Amherst."

"Really?"

"I have to," she said. "My college loans. I promised I'd earn money this summer. So far I've saved seventeen dollars."

"What if you stopped buying cigarettes?"

"What if you shut up."

He laughed. "Well, you know my finances are a mess, too. I started with a thousand dollars for the summer and I'm already on the brink of starvation. I wonder if I could work at Amherst, too. Maybe—"

"Scooter, you always have much more money than you let on. Don't play with me."

"No, really."

"Scooter, that'd be *great*."

"I need the printmaking studio anyway."

"We'd have the best time."

Silence.

"What would you say to Gill?"

"Something."

"Careful."

"Mmm. I'll write to Lillian for housing. But this phone call is very expensive."

"Who's getting billed?"

"My mom, actually. I used her billing number. But I do pay her back most of the time."

"Sure . . ." Then she whispered softly, "Meantime, *pommes de terre Anna*, asparagus, endive salad, béarnaise sauce . . ."

"Shut up. I miss you."

"Of course you do."

The next morning, from the lobby of the Art Students' League, James wrote Lillian Gilder, secretary of fine arts, a postcard.

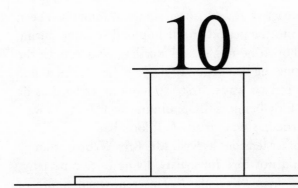

# 10

At nineteen, Guillaume Brix-Webber often worried that his life lacked focus. To others it may not have seemed so: with his intent gaze, his very intellectual bearing (his spectacles, most visibly) and his habit of closing in quite rapidly on anyone or anything that interested him, he actually impressed contemporaries with an air of myopic concentration upon the affairs of his own life. Oblivious to circumstances that took place beyond his range of vision or outside his areas of interest, he was often referred to, with a shrug, as an unbearably "directed" undergraduate. Certainly he did tend to get what he wanted once it had aroused his interest. Only (and few perceived this, for he was hesitant to disclose anything that might be perceived as a weakness) he had always had trouble deciding what he wanted. And apart from an early decision to be the man who sliced salami at the butcher store (made at a tender age, in the company of his housekeeper), he had never had a clear idea of how he wanted to spend his life. Recently he had begun to feel apprehensive about this lack of occupational drive. People around him had begun to specialize.

In the hope of deciding on a vocation, he had arranged a conspicuously inactive and antisocial summer. James had been a late exception to the period of self-imposed solitude during which he had hoped he might find a calling. Now, with the summer half gone, he had begun to despair. James had added to this anxiety in two ways: first, by working as hard as he did, and second, by being as disappointing an artist as he was. Both, in its particular way, made Gill look bad.

There were other tensions as well. Mr. Brix-Webber, though he loved art, did not care for artists, living ones especially, for he thought them "irregular." This renowned figure of international finance was also a recluse, or at least had made a lifelong point of keeping his house free of overnight guests. James knew nothing of this, and Gill, extraordinarily gracious by nature, had gone to great lengths to keep the knowledge from him, as well as to keep his father from ever meeting his guest.

But Gill was also aware of his failure as a teacher with James, and now acknowledged, if only to himself, that he had taken on James' project out of what could also be described as blind enthusiasm. In the past two weeks he had begun to appreciate both the project's difficulties and his friend's limitations. Still, he had no desire to hurt James' feelings. Though they were not close, they had been living together amicably, and were in fact about to meet for dinner and an opening.

Gill sighed, shifting from one foot to another, lost in thought. He had been waiting outside the Art Students' League a good fifteen minutes, alternately surveying the window displays and the building itself, only marginally aware of the people streaming past him toward the subway. He had been interested, though, in the students leaving the building, catching as they passed a draught of the damp air coming out with them, air whose smell (musty, tired, flavored with turpentine and cigars, plate oil and printing ink) appealed to him as the hint of an answer: a substantial smell, as simple and moving, he decided, as that of baking bread.

Moving closer to the doorway, hands in pockets, he took another breath, catching again that something he wanted to be near. Art was being made puzzling deliberately, perhaps also a trifle self-consciously (he was wearing a new shirt) over the sensations drifting over him and through him on this late summer afternoon, he stood a few moments longer and then, thinking he was being watched, turned around.

Far down Fifty-seventh Street, the sign above Duane Reade flashed five-forty-seven and ninety-three degrees; nobody had been looking at him.

"Hey, Gill."

A smudged, bleary-eyed James spoke from the top of the landing, where he had caught his plastic shopping bag in the double doors. His preoccupied expression—fatigue, mostly —made Gill, in his aloof way, somewhat melancholy.

"Been waiting long?"

"No."

James acknowledged his friend's look of vague amusement, and the two shook hands.

"What's in the bag?"

James opened it to display orange peels, a Tab can, charcoal, his journal and ledger, and an aerosol container of spray fixative.

Gill nodded gravely, then removed the Tab can and threw it in a nearby trash heap. James watched him and, when he came back, said, "Gill, I usually return those for the five cents."

"Sorry."

"That's okay." They stood a moment looking at each other. "I left the drawings in my locker since we were going out. They're safer . . . are you all right?"

"Mmmm . . . Yes, of course."

James nodded.

"Well, actually, James, I've been watching this place for the past twenty minutes and it's really nothing like I'd imagined. People here don't seem very bohemian."

"They really aren't."

"This place, more than any other in the city, represents to me the possibilities of Art for the People, Art whose specific concern is with the lives of ordinary people. But to tell the truth it never occurred to me that people here would be quite so . . . ordinary."

"Hmm. Ever been in?"

"No, actually."

They walked up the steps.

"The art's pretty ordinary, too."

Back outside, Gill looked down the street, which was piled with garbage, backed up with traffic, and crowded with people swarming toward the subway. The day showed no sign of ending. "This is disgusting," he said. He had not been impressed with the lobby of the Art Students' League.

"Try drawing out here sometime."

They looked at each other.

"Drinks."

"There's a good place around here," James said. "An artists' hangout, sort of, I like to think."

"What kind—?"

"Well . . . I don't know, really. I mean, it's run by Greeks, but I don't know if you could go so far as to call it a Greek restaurant. You'll see."

"I have money." Gill said weakly.

"No, really. You'll love this place."

A grime-encrusted sign over a gaping doorway on West Fifty-eighth Street announced their arrival at the Athena III coffee shop. The dark, busy place, lit by sputtering candles in dusty, wax-covered Chianti bottles, was evidently under joint management by three hairy men who hated each other. The three argued ferociously as they waited on tables.

"Athena means 'cheap' in Greek." James chuckled. "All four Athena coffee shops are great. There's one up by me on Moshulu Parkway. Killer doughnuts. You'll love it."

Gill smiled. Otherwise familiar with the area, he had never before noticed this restaurant, tucked as it was behind and below another much more expensive. Passing the cash register he looked for, but did not find, a certification from the board of health.

They sat in a booth.

"This was the first place I ever got really drunk," James said. He was sweating. "I came here after the Picasso press opening at MOMA. My friend had passes from her mom. We got so wasted."

Gill looked again at his friend. Then he gazed deferentially at his spotty menu, which he held close beneath their sputtering, large but rapidly melting candle. The heat in the room was intense. They were one booth away from the kitchen, and the sound of plates being lifted, dropped, and cursed over was formidable.

"We stayed late drinking," James concluded, "until they played bouzouki music on the stereo and fed us leftover cheese."

Gill adjusted his glasses and said, "James, you certainly know your way around."

His friend acknowledged the compliment with a nod.

"What's good?"

"I like the American cheese omelet," James said. "But there's a special that includes wine."

The waiter, the heaviest of the three, stopped arguing momentarily to demand their order. On James' recommendation they had the special, which was a large pitcher of jug wine with some whitish cheese and an apple. They drank the wine from jelly jars and when the first pitcher was empty another replaced it. Picking the wax off the table and the bottle, James dropped bits into the sputtering flame, talking about life in general, and, eventually, his anatomy class in particular.

"Then there's Henry . . . he has problems with the rest of the class, but he's very good. He's the midget. And then George, who works hard, but I get the feeling he's going to go back into real estate soon unless he gets discovered. He's never sold a drawing. Then there's a really really old guy who comes to class to try to pick people up. It's kind of funny, because he doesn't even bother to bring a pencil or pad with him. George tells me he's been enrolled in the course for years. Then . . . well, let's see. There's Crystal and Vanessa, who are friends. They both quit publishing about the same time to illustrate children's books. They're in the course because they Lack the Basic Skills, as they put it. But to tell the truth, there aren't as many good draughtsmen enrolled as I'd hoped. I'm pretty sure there are no real artists there except Henry, and he keeps to himself. Like I said. Sometimes, though, if I stop in here after work, I'll see him and say hello.

Gill listened, nodding, as James went on to talk about Gloria, whose bosom posed a great and almost unresolvable problem. Then about other strangely shaped models: the ballet dancer who was missing her front teeth; the short, bandy-legged Spanish couple; the juggling bodybuilder who did shorter poses standing on his hands, thereby creating extraordinary problems of foreshortening and perspective. Gloria was by far the easiest to get right on paper.

They continued all the while to drink and eat cheese. With the second and third pitcher the dark room became more congenial, the surrounding roar settled into a dull buzz, and in the deep booth each put his feet up beside the other. Gill answered James' questions about the art world as best he could, speaking briefly, if vaguely, about his own interest in collecting art, and then about Rupert Boynton.

"Boynton really makes art today," he said. "Or at least decides who gets bought. Wonderful man, very strange." He trailed off. "I went to Dalton with Yvonne Boynton."

James nodded with interest, munching down the last piece of cheese.

"Most artists have problems surviving in the real world. They need good collectors and good dealers to find them and take care of them."

James nodded again, then brightened. "Hey, look . . . that's Henry. He just came in."

Gill looked over quickly. Henry was sitting alone, scribbling in a book.

"Please excuse," James said. "Nature calls."

He returned to an empty table. A moment later he spotted Gill chatting amicably with Henry in the corner. Henry pointed to James, Gill jotted something quickly into his pocket notebook, and, before James could join him, returned to the booth.

"Nice man," Gill said.

"Geez, he really talked to you," James said. "He never talks to anybody."

"I have a way with little people."

"Gill, I never know when to take you seriously."

Another waiter, short and bald, brought coffee, returning momentarily with a leftover dessert for free. "On de 'ouse," he said. "For friend of 'Enrys."

Gill turned and waved to Henry. James noticed that the three waiters now seemed to be fighting about the dessert, each gesticulating wildly toward their booth. Though neither Gill nor James ate the dessert, they did have the good sense to order another pitcher of wine. Another argument soon drew the waiters away from them.

"Isn't this place great?" James asked, sitting back, his face and neck slightly flushed.

Gill shrugged, but in a way that indicated he liked it. When the time came both left very large tips. James explained that he had already overspent his evening's budget but, resolving to economize in the coming weeks, figured it was okay.

Stumbling up onto the sidewalk, they were greatly surprised to find the sun up and people walking about as if work had just ended. They squinted at one another.

"Cab?" Gill said.

"Walk?"

In the cab, James broke the lull in conversation to talk about his financial situation, even though his throat was tired.

"I mean," he said, "I'm really just hanging in there. I'm pretty sure I'll make it through the summer if I continue to live carefully. I've decided that economy is my biggest challenge this summer."

Gill nodded, looking out of the window.

There was plenty of time to look at the new shops on West Broadway before going to the gallery. In one of them, Gill admired and eventually bought a lapis tie clip. At the fifth shop they went into, James said, "Gee, Gill, you really know your way around."

Gill nodded, wide-eyed in agreement, pushing his glasses rather knowingly up the bridge of his nose.

The opening was one of many to which Gill's parents received invitations but did not attend. The art was unfamiliar to both of them and Gill recognized only a few people. He said a dutiful hello to anyone he knew but, unsure of names, did not introduce his friend. After some small talk James got some wine at the far end of the room while Gill picked up a listing and poked through the catalogue. After taking as many notes as he needed in his small notebook, he rejoined James, telling him briefly what was going on.

"Is anybody here from the art world?" James asked.

"James," Gill said, "This *is* the art world."

"Oh. Right."

"But no, nobody really notable. That man is pretty well known for his collection of surrealists," he said, pointing. "I think he's a dentist. The couple over there owns a house near ours in Sagaponack. That woman runs a gallery as a tax shelter for her husband, who makes too much money in New York real estate."

"Oh."

Just as both were unenthused by the guest list, neither was particularly taken with the art, which consisted of splotches of gesso, lipstick, and library paste over paper and masonite board.

"Untitled, too, I hope you noticed," James said.

"I'm curious," Gill said. "Tell me what you think."

"Sure," he answered. "I don't like 'em."

Gill looked ahead blankly, waiting for more, then glanced quickly up at James to see if he had, in fact, finished. James shrugged.

113

"Well—why?"

"I just don't."

"I see." Gill looked at him again, moving in closer. "Do you resent the predominance of the so-called neo-Expressionist impulses—the heavy impasto, the massing of difficult color passages across the picture plane, the violent tonalities of the painting? Or is it the use of Modernist collage in a work that really undercuts the Modernist tradition . . . a semiotic objection? Or perhaps you think it relies too heavily on allusion to make its point. Is it insincere, invalid, or just tired?"

"Gee, I don't know," James said at last. "I mean, I usually just go with my feelings on this sort of stuff. It does seem pretty tired, though, now that you mention it."

Gill nodded.

They wandered through the room, then decided while talking to each other through a hollowed-out sculpture that they should leave. Both had had too much wine to want to stand up much longer. Just as they were about to go, James asked Gill, "I think I'll take some cheese for lunch tomorrow. Nobody here's eating much. Think it's okay?"

"I don't see why not," Gill said reasonably. "Here. I'll cover for you."

They drifted toward the refreshment table. Gill caught the eye of the gallery assistant and directed her attention to the catalogue, questioning her while James leaned over behind him and with a deft motion lifted a pound and a half of Jarlsberg and dropped it into his shopping bag. He then turned to Gill, tapped his shoulder, and out the door they went.

Halfway to Greene Street, they saluted the success of the opening with a "high-five."

Gill pointed out a number of famous galleries as they headed uptown. They made their next stop at a record store, then went into a bar, where Gill played video games for a long time. His reflexes were poor because he had become extremely drunk. They sat at the bar after spending six dollars on the machines.

After buying the second round James opened his journal to record the latest installments of the evening's expenditures. "Sheesh," he said, staring at the column of numbers. "Gill, I really, really blew it tonight. Look at all this."

Gill shrugged.

"But I guess I feel pretty okay about it, too. I mean—"

"That journal," Gill said, squinting at it and leaning heavily on James' shoulder to see what it looked like up close. "What's in there anyway?"

He reached slowly for it and knocked over his drink.

"Whoa, Gill baby. Steady, boy."

"Let me see it."

"You'd *destroy* it. You'd spill stuff *all over* it."

"*Give it to me.*"

"No."

James wiped up the drink.

"You can't say no to your host."

He considered this statement. "All right, what the hell."

Gill took the book and flipped rapidly through pages of drawings (still lifes, landscapes, portraits), found objects, shopping lists, and assorted written observations.

"There's nothing about you," James said.

"I don't take it personally."

"Good of you."

He stopped to look at a rather detailed drawing of the 231st Street elevated subway platform.

"The places you *go*," he said. "Where is 231st Street?"

"Kingsbridge. On *Broadway*. Don't you know *Broadway*?"

"Broadway doesn't go to the Bronx."

"Of *course* it does." James looked at him. "It goes to *Yonkers,* imbecile."

That ended the conversation for a while. Gill ordered the next round and James took back his book and drew Gill.

"Cheers."

"Hmm," Gill said. "That's not very good."

Crossing Houston, they walked over to Broadway, then up Broadway to Great Jones, then down Great Jones over to the Bowery, where a drunk lay snoring in a doorway.

"I think we've found your next drawing, James."

James nodded and belched. Gill stepped over the drunk; James made a great point of walking deliberately around him.

"I know you deal with people like that every day, Gill," James said, "but look what you just did. You could have *stepped* on him."

Gill looked reasonably from James to the man. "Yes, but I didn't."

"But you *could* have."

"I *didn't,* though."

"Well, some day you *might.* Then you'd be sorry."

"Some day *you* might. I won't."

"Well, look. All I'm going to say is that you could remember every once in a while that this is your fellow man. That's all I have to say to you. I'm not going to push the point. He is your fellow man."

Gill looked down. "Damn right. Give him the cheese."

"*What?*"

"You heard me."

"It's *my* cheese."

"He's *your* fellow man, too."

"Yes, but it's *my* cheese."

"It's our cheese. Give it to him."

**116**

"It was *my* lunch." He glared at Gill. "Indian giver."

"Latent petty bourgeois capitalist adventurer."

The man at their feet stopped snoring.

"Now you've said it."

"Sorry. Both of you."

James did not say anything for a long time. When he did speak, it was in a low, even tone.

"He can have the cheese. Think of it as my first and last performance piece."

He tore a piece of paper from his journal and laid the cheese on it before the sleeping man. "There," he said, "I call it, 'Art for Breakfast.' "

" 'Art for *Lunch*,' " Gill said, adding by way of explanation, "He looks like he sleeps late."

"I don't like 'Art for Lunch.' "

"But it's catchy. Think about it."

"Art for Lunch." James said. "Art for Lunch. Art for Lunch."

As the bed rolled and pitched him about that evening, James thought about his lunch a great deal. The cheese stood alone on Great Jones Street; three men argued in Greek, flourishing dish towels and cutlery; a shower of pennies (surely enough to buy a bag of hazelnut cookies) cascaded from a tenement roof, tumbling in sparkles past buzzy streetlamps, disappearing, lost, into an ominous din of hi-tech percussion on sidewalk and trash cans below.

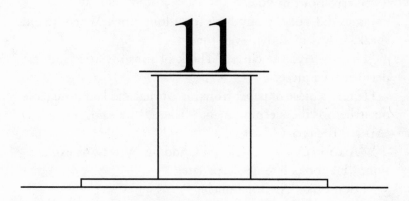

# 11

It was the Fourth of July. Gill and Dolly, nestling at the tiny kitchen table, settled into a day's work in front of Brix-Webber's mini-TV. Earlier, Dolly had made eggs that Gill refused to eat because she had not removed the white strandy things. Instead they drank tea and ate mango. On this, the morning of finals, he was in rare form: wearing his best tennis togs, he had stacked before him his magazines, a blank notebook, a pen, a scorecard, and an autographed Wimbledon souvenir program from the year before. But while he relied upon the finals (Connors and McEnroe) for entertainment, he was actually quite busy sorting through a number of gallery guides, catalogues, and reproductions; for he had set the day aside to catch up on art homework.

Dolly, for her part, watched Gill and mended a shirt, eager to provide company and refreshment. During the commercials they spoke some, but, hard at it since half-past eight, not much. Somewhere into the first set, James slid down the marble hall and into the kitchen, whistling.

"Morning!"

"Hi, James."

James patted Gill on the head, looked at the TV, jumped up and down like a tennis player, then tapped with his fingers upon the different appliances and set the kettle to boil. Since there was no more room at the table, he leant against the counter to drink his instant coffee, tapping with a spoon upon several empty glasses. At the commercial, Dolly turned warily to him and said,

"Too much of dat give you boils."

James nodded. Gill raised his tea and nodded too.

"Today's got to have it."

Then they all looked out the window to see what kind of day it was.

"Hot out . . . I played a set early," Gill said. "But it's a cool eighty-five in Wimbledon."

The tennis returned.

"I think McEnroe's going to win. I have his autograph. . . . See?"

He handed James the notebook without turning around. James nodded, put it down, and sipped his coffee. The room quieted to sounds of tennis, then a cheer.

"Art homework?"

"Mmm."

"Guess I'll get going . . . Want to—"

"Think it's straight sets?"

"Beats me. . . . I'll be out on the mall if you want me, okay? Drawing."

"Mmm."

James went to the study window and gazed down sideways to Fifth Avenue and the park beyond. On waking an exhilaration had seized him of a sort other than coffee; churning and pumping within was something that had been missing for weeks. Excitement: the Fourth of July. The summer was, for this one day at least, something of an event. Today was bound to be interesting.

The intersection at Fifth was completely deserted. A stillness rare even at this time of year had invaded the neighborhood; nothing moving and nobody anywhere. The ice cream truck on the corner, torrid heat, the humid smell of sidewalks, the overwhelming quiet viewed from above: summer holiday in an empty city. The park would be different. On weekends like this the outlying boroughs invaded by subway and weirdos came out of their basements to sprawl on the grass.

"The mall, Gill."

The words rallied him into action: lacing up sneakers, grabbing the art bag, he called good-bye down the long marble hall and elevated down to the cool glass lobby. Going out he was met with a blast of hot, sticky air, but it got a bit cooler inside the park.

He started off with three views of the Bethesda fountain. The place was deserted; people sat in the shade off the pavilion drinking sodas; in the hazy glare of midmorning sun, the shadows were weak and diffuse. The view was flat and unconvincing and so were his first attempts at drawing.

"Blech."

After leaping up the stairs, two by two, he turned at the top to look back once more, but the light was still bad, all glare. Next came the mall: more benches, more people, and more shade. People were hard at work putting something together at the band shell. Hot dog stands sat abandoned down a quarter-mile stretch of hexagonal paving stones, watched over by statues as their proprietors lounged in the shade. Radios blared music from under trees. No one moved. On the Sheep Meadow side, apart from them, stood an easel with drawings spread round it.

James had never seen an artist set up on the mall before. He decided to investigate.

The drawings were arranged across the bench and on the pavement before it: pastel on newsprint, bright-spirited, pathetically rendered portraits. A cardboard sign announced, "Drawing three dollars." Close by, his hair full of lint, the zipper on his pants tenuously secured with a safety pin, a man lay dozing. His clothes were very badly stained and he had a large pile of rubbish at his feet. His eyes, when they opened, were crossed; the duller of the two watered incessantly, tearing down one cheek. Seeing James, he sat up and rubbed his face with his hands.

"Want a portrait?"

"Did you do these?"

The man nodded. James looked at the drawings, which were very primitive, and nodded approvingly, feeling the bum (or now, rather, the artist, he thought) look at him.

James sat down on the bench and took out some of his own drawings, which looked very tame by comparison.

"Want painting lessons?" the man asked hopefully. "Five dollars a hour."

"No."

"Three."

"No thanks."

"Two."

James flipped through more drawings.

The man moved closer to look at the drawings.

"You only do things in black and white. That's crazy. You could put lots of color there. I could teach you."

"Well, thank you, but it's part of a project."

"A little color look fine with that."

He shrugged.

"That's a pity," the man said, shaking his head slowly and cleaning his ear with his finger. "Sure is a pity . . . but I guess it's more classical your way, right? . . . like, Raphael."

James looked up.

"Hello, Raphael. James. How do you do."

"No, man. My name is Richard. Raphael is the artist."

"Right . . . sorry."

James began sketching. Richard watched, for a moment interested, then settled back again, amused, and ate some potato chips from a wrinkled bag.

"Maybe . . . drawin' like this all day, we get some business," he said slowly, eyeing James. "Or maybe at the museum you could get more, what you think. I would personally like to get some money."

"But all the museums are closed today."

"Closed?"

"It's the Fourth of July. . . . Right here's okay."

"It's empty."

"Gets crowded." James looked at Richard and began another sketch, this time including him in the foreground. Suddenly he was drawing well. "Have you been doing this a long time?"

Richard said he had not.

He, too, was from the Bronx.

"Nobody up there's gonna buy a drawing," he said. "They think I'm crazy. I got to make a living at it, so I come downtown where there's money and the museums to try it out.

This' my first month. Subway's expensive so I don't know. Maybe I *am* crazy. People sellin' weed all I found here yet —sellin' weed. Smoke some weed?" Richard paused. James shrugged and continued sketching. "People always tell me, 'Try the museum at the park, people there like art, they buy anything.' Hah."

James had the presence of mind to ask, "Which museum?"

"One on the park."

"Where?"

"By the subway?"

James stopped sketching. "Well, the IND lets you off at the Museum of Natural History. People don't sell art there. People sell art on the other side, at the Metropolitan Museum."

Richard looked at James. "No *shit*."

"No."

"Let's go."

"But it's closed."

"Sure?"

"Very sure."

"Oh."

They sat awhile saying nothing. James drew. People were beginning to appear.

"Okay . . . almost finished."

He held it up: a good drawing. "I think I messed up the eye."

"You got the eye wrong . . . or right," Richard laughed. "You know, this is artificial."

"Really?"

"Yeah." Richard said smiling. "Look at the sparkles. Ready?" Richard put his hand to his eye and with a quick scooping motion pulled it out. The false eye, like a prize marble, had bits of metallic glitter in it.

"God. How did you do that?"

"Gotta bottle throwed at me." Richard said, looking at his bad eye with his good eye. "It's good for drawing people 'cause they don't know you're lookin' at 'em if you cross-eyed."

James considered the statement. "I guess it comes in handy."

"That's a nice drawing. Put it on the bench. Now's my turn."

James put down his pad. Richard pushed his eye back in place, and then stood to prepare his easel. A group of people came by and pointed at the drawing and at some of the portraits on the ground, then left. Richard's easel was rickety and the paper kept coming unstuck; he spent a good deal of time offering to do portraits of the people passing by.

"I got to get paying customers, you see," he said loudly, not really to James.

Then he decided it was time for souvlaki. After haggling with several vendors, he returned with a large, very sloppy sandwich that dribbled on his newsprint and several of his drawings. Sauce fell into the box of pastels.

"What's new?" Richard asked, licking souvlaki from the side of his hand. "Who are you, man?"

James turned, surprised. A man had approached and sat beside the drawings next to him. He had a crew cut, several day's growth of beard, a puka shell necklace, an orange T-shirt that said "Florida," and black polyester pants. On his feet were ragged yellow flip-flops. One big toe was bloody and crusted with dirt.

The stranger mumbled and smiled and as Richard set to work explained in very soft, mixed-up English he was from Argentina, that his name was Carlos, that he'd come to hear a concert and stubbed his toe. Richard offered him the potato chips bag. Carlos shook his head politely. Then Richard decided to find an open bathroom and a phone and left, stopping halfway across the mall, James noticed, to share what looked like a joint with another man who looked rather like him. Meanwhile, James showed Carlos the drawings he'd done. A baby carriage pushed by a hoarse-whispering old man creaked up the mall. The carriage dripped steadily, leaving a dark trail of water on the gray pavement. Passing them he said, "*Cerveza fria.*"

And Carlos looked up in surprise. James thought he'd try to draw the man but he was moving too quickly. Then another old man, fat and shirtless, walked toward them from another direction carrying shopping bags. He sat on the end of their bench in the sunlight, closing his eyes. James sketched him. Carlos watched with interest, and at last said, "Almost."

James looked up at Carlos and then returned to his sketch. Richard returned from the band shell.

"It's closed."

"The bathroom?"

"The museum."

"Well, it's picking up here," James said. I don't really think you have to move, Richard, really."

Richard nodded.

A pudgy mime chalked out a circle in front of them. The day was hot but no longer still; the air had begun to stir, swelling gently with sounds of laughter and music, smells of grilling shish kabobs and new-mown grass. Richard went back to doing James' portrait and a crowd gathered to watch. The mime bought a soda and came to stand in the shade beside them. Across the way, people had assembled to watch the show at the band shell. A troupe of Norwegian Girl Scouts, some carrying flags, now performed a salute to America by marching in place to "Nadia's Theme."

Carlos smiled and clapped, his expression decidedly odd.

Richard continued lackadaisically with the portrait. To pass the time, James drew Carlos watching the girls at the band shell.

He held the drawing up to show Richard.

"That's fine. . . . Good perspective. Very fine."

Carlos nodded enthusiastically. "Almost."

Then Carlos rose and wandered toward the band shell. The mime began to perform; people turned from them to watch him. In a few minutes Carlos came back with three beers, handing one to Richard and one to James. "*Salud.*"

James said, "Thank you."

Richard said, "It's done," and then, popping his can open, "Arright." He stood back. "You could come check out your portrait now."

James stood to look. The face was drawn flat and head-on in peach-colored pastel, touched up in places with a cosmetic sensibility: cheeks rouged bright pink, eyes rimmed with charcoal, tiny mouth painted rosebud-red, the hair outlined in black, then filled in strand by strand with streaks of yellow and brown. The whole thing was connected by a long, stem-like neck to a brilliant purple, green, and orange plaid shirt.

The three looked at it a long time, nodding. Carlos poked James in the ribs and smiled. "Almost."

Richard nodded. "Long as you enjoyed doing it, that's all that's important," he said. "Then you're a good artist. Long as you enjoyed it, it's fine what you do."

They drank to the successful completion of the drawing, which Richard posted as an ad.

"Don't go 'way. People want drawings if they see it looks like you."

James, who had only had coffee, began to feel lightheaded from the beer, and bought the next round.

*  *  *

Gill had finished his art homework before the last set. Wimbledon had ended by twelve, with McEnroe winning more quickly than anyone had predicted, leaving Gill to wander up and down the hall with a sense of anticlimax so strong it verged on abandonment. All the art this summer was unspeakably dull. The last set had been a *fait accompli*. Nothing Pat Somerall could say would make it better.

He walked to his room and changed, then walked to the study and stared out the window, then walked to his mother's room to look at the cable movies schedule. Then he made a small lunch. He called a few friends but, predictably, none were home. After looking at the *Times* and deciding there were no good movies, he decided to go out, he didn't know where. Maybe the park.

He would probably never find James. There was such a distance between them, anyway. It was unfair of a houseguest to keep so much to himself. Changing into shorts, a T-shirt, sunglasses, and a straw hat, he called, "Good-bye, Dolly, I'm off on a mission of espionage," and, safely disguised, headed out to the park.

Back at the mall the day gathered momentum; the haze had burned off and the light was clearer, the weather less humid. People stood in clusters, some watching Richard; behind, on Sheep Meadow, others lay out in bikinis and Ray-Bans, tanning and gossiping and listening to radios; between the mall and the meadow roller skaters milled and spun around boxes blaring rap music. Some without wheels danced with the skaters, while others stood watching, whispering and laughing with each other. On the mall proper, jazz groups and a steel drum band had set up; the Norwegians had disappeared into a schoolbus. Richard, meanwhile, had negotiated a group portrait of a Puerto Rican family, who after some haggling settled on a price of three dollars, which Richard made them pay in advance; now he was hard at work. There were nine of them. The first thing they had wanted on paper was the family name, which was "Ledesma."

James and Carlos went off to watch the bands, and stayed at the steel drums a long time. They returned to an argument. A number of spectators, some in hats, sunglasses, or roller skates, stood by listening with interest.

Richard was about half finished with the drawing of the family; a boy in a purple shirt and maroon shorts, his face sticky with ice cream, had interrupted him in his work.

"You made that lady look like a dog . . . look at that nose there. . . . Why don't you use a camera? Huh, mister? That way it'd look more like 'em and it wouldn't cost three bucks. It'd cost a lot cheaper and then it'd look like 'em."

"It wouldn't be the same."

"It'd *look* more like 'em."

"That's not Art."

"But it'd look more like 'em. She looks like a dog."

"Pictures ain't Art."

"It don't cost no three bucks to take no picture. Pictures are cheaper and they don't make you look like no dog."

At the urgent prompting of his wife, the man on the bench approached the easel, and looking at it with concern said, "He right. No look like us."

"See, I told ya."

Richard stood up straight. "It's Art."

"It's a portrait, no? A portrait got to look like us."

Richard shrugged and set back to work. The man grumbled but returned to the bench. In another ten minutes the drawing was done and the family gathered frowning to look at it, muttering among themselves as they left. The grand-mother rolled the portrait, flattened it, and stuck it in a bulky string bog.

"Where's the pool?" the mother asked James.

"Way up," James said, pointing.

The family walked out of sight, all of them muttering, none looking back.

Nobody wanted portraits after that. Richard asked James about drawing landscapes. James showed some of his and tried to say what he thought was good about them. Richard shook his head.

"I got a hard time doing *portraits*," he said. "I ain't doing no *landscape*. Nobody gonna pay for no *landscape*."

The mime did his performance seven times. Each perform-ance ended when the mime hung himself with a piece of imaginary rope. Richard and James and Carlos clapped each time it ended. Then, when James bought a six-pack, they closed up for the afternoon and sat talking. Richard hoped someday to have an exhibition at the Museum of the Bronx on Grand Concourse. He wanted to teach art for a living but needed certification and that meant going to school. He couldn't do that, because he had to support himself, but was trying to figure something out.

A bald man asked for a portrait but said two dollars was too much. Richard glared at him, then stood and wrote *Closed* on his easel.

"You come here often?" James asked.

"Hell no. I ain't never coming back after *today*."

"Why?"

Richard looked at James as if he was crazy. "I gotta find a place where I can get customers. Gotta be a place where an artist could sell a drawing."

"Yeah," James said.

**129**

"Maybe the museum. Depends if I got enough for the subway. Artist leads a hard life."

"It is the only way," Carlos said.

Richard nodded. Carlos nodded. James nodded. They watched the mime once more and then James stood up, lost his balance, sat down, then stood up again.

"Well, maybe I'll see you at the museum."

"Maybe."

"Good luck in America, Carlos."

"Yes," Carlos said, "yes."

Then he shook Carlos' hand. Somebody tapped him on the shoulder.

"Hey, James."

James turned, trying to recognize the short person in sombrero and wraparound sunglasses.

"Gill?"

"Who are your friends?" Gill took off the glasses. He looked very pleased with himself.

"This is Richard and Carlos," James said. "Is everything okay?"

"Sure. Hi."

Richard and Carlos waved. James wobbled a bit, and squinted at Gill through one eye.

"How long have you been here?"

"A while."

"You missed a good party, man," Richard said.

"Oh, yeah," said Carlos. James was bright red.

On the walk home Gill asked about Richard and Carlos. James offered him some of the last beer, which he declined, and asked Gill in turn what he had thought of them.

"The possibilities of art for the common man live on in him," Gill said. "He strikes me as heroic. I only wish more people in our society could find satisfaction and fulfillment in the visual arts. Just think how much richer our society would be."

They crossed out of the 76th Street gate onto Fifth Avenue, walking south under the plane trees.

"I know," James said. "It *is* neat. But didn't he look pretty bummy?"

Gill looked puzzled.

"Bummy . . . *bummy*. You know—like a bum. Not everybody can be like a bum, Gill. I mean, I know I've done my best this summer but I just don't think I have enough bumminess to do it full time. I just want you to know that. That, and that I'm sorry. I really am."

Gill noticed that his friend had suddenly gone from bright red to pale green, and took the art bag from him, supporting him with one arm.

"James—did you have much to drink?"

"I dunno. I feel kind of . . . baaaargh."

Gill watched his friend with incredulity. "What an extraordinary life he leads," he said later, to Dolly.

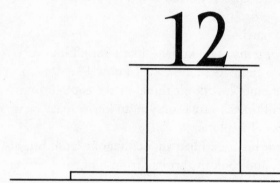

## 12

Mrs. Brix-Webber's bedroom, the only room in the Brix-Webber apartment with any sort of view, had gradually, with the advance of art and collectibles through the formal and semiformal rooms of the house, become the family's (and lately, James') main living space. Summer afternoons here were truly breathtaking. A cold breeze rose routinely off the park at around four, stirring the long, light curtains at the front of the room and bringing with it the scent of cut grass and cool leaves. Bright rays of late sun mingled with the glow of the silenced Magnavox. Stacks of mail, books, and papers sat in neat piles on the thick white rugs and stray furniture, waiting attentively to be picked up and browsed through. Gill had been spending an awful lot of time here lately.

Today he was crosslegged in the middle of the bed reading a very large picture book, *The Triumph of American Painting*. With Peanut lying beside him breathing heavily, and with his glasses slowly but surely making their way to the end of his nose, he looked smaller and more childlike than usual. He was not really reading, just flipping through the pictures.

Rather edgily he pushed his glasses up the bridge of his nose and looked up. Then he closed the book, marking his place with a postcard from Rupert Boynton of Boynton-Crest, and selected a chocolate to feed the dog.

Peanut took the piece gently from his hand, consuming it with small grunting noises. Gill watched, trying to locate the exact source of the noise.

The summer was not going as well as he had planned.

For the past three weeks he had tried, unsuccessfully, to start his friend off on a career in the arts. He had managed (by lending James the family membership passes and giving him the names of people to meet) to get him to some of the important museums and art galleries. But none of these explorations seemed to have provoked much interest or insight—or, for that matter, good conversation. All that had really set James off had been a show of WPA etchings at the Triple-A—not the most exciting stuff. Instead, James talked every night about the weird things that happened when he drew on the street. Granted, a few of his experiences had been extraordinary. But while he might wander adventurously through places one only heard of in the *Post* (Dolly received it; the whole family read it), James had an exceptional talent for making even the extraordinary mundane. Gill had been surprised to learn how difficult it was to do art of his sort well, and surprised again at the lack of interest the art itself could arouse. James' landscapes and street scenes were academic: well-composed, well-lit, full of significant form. But they were not much else. They would not give comfort to the masses; nor would they foment a people's revolution.

He put the book aside, uncrossed his legs, and reached

again for the yellow pad. He had been trying to write his novel all day. Morning had been set aside for titles, noon for outlines, afternoon for rough drafts. He was writing a testimonial of his work in the soup kitchen and had settled, around eleven, on his title: *The Bowl Half-Full*. It had, he thought, a nicely Rilkean air.

He had quit his job at the soup kitchen over a week ago to devote himself to writing. Unfortunately he could only write so much in a day and, once done, he had so little else to do. Around noon he had spoken to Chantal, his friend in L.A., who had been most enthusiastic on the book's possibilities as a documentary, or perhaps even a screenplay. It had great potential and atmosphere. Now all he had to do was finish it.

But New York in summer was no place for Gill. All his friends were away. He had taken his summer position in the soup kitchen knowing he would be alone and that in this relative seclusion he could begin his first work. Then he had left the kitchen to write full time. With too much time on his hands, Gill had found James a welcome diversion. But James' project had been a disappointment and now, despite Gill's rather formidable connections to Interesting People throughout the city, he was without friends, without regular employment, and all but lacking in artistic inspiration that could outlast the morning. As of today the manuscript was ten and a half heavily revised pages long. (He was not counting the title page, opening quotation, or table of contents.)

He had stopped going out in the evenings because he could rarely find anyone to do something with. While James was a suitable enough companion, he rarely wanted to spend money on going out. Moreover, he looked so tired when he came back from his inexplicable street wanderings, and somewhat wary of his host as well. Why this was so Gill could not understand; he was trying not to take it personally.

He had other thoughts about it. There was always an air of contention between them: James was either quietly dismissive (usually the case when discussing Central American politics) or else head-up and exasperated (especially concerning comparative aesthetic philosophies). Gill did not mind disagreement *per se*: dialectical reasoning was in fact, for him, a way of life. But James did not disagree, he sulked, and his opinions, once expressed, were frequently illogical and often (though Gill hated to admit it, even to himself) boring.

Peanut yawned.

"What to do, sweet pea?"

Gill rose up in defiance of boredom. He stretched and did a little tai-chi; he went to the kitchen and drank some seltzer with lemon; he did ten pushups on the marble floor in the hallway. He returned to his mother's room and stood on his head to watch television. Then he retrieved his address book and began to update it by calling every number to find out if the people he had listed were still at the numbers he had written. Twelve of the first thirteen calls were not answered.

Then he had a brainstorm: dialing direct to Antibes, he began to track down his mother, who would, he knew, be starting out on one of her late evenings. He wished it was evening in New York.

Four calls later he had brought her to bay in a restaurant near the hotel. After a few moments of slurred midi French, the voice—low, cool, and silvered, through the years, with the smoke of many cigarettes—rang distinctively over the ocean.

"Hul-lo-oo?"

Gill said, "Mommy."

"*Zut!* My darling child?"

"Yes. Hello."

"Set it there . . . that's fine. Darling, it's so sweet of you to call. Hello back. Hold as Mommy gets the lovely waiter to light her cigarette and brings *une autre*."

Gill's mother was neither English nor French, but she had with time acquired a certain proficiency with a limited number of phrases and mannerisms of each, which made her seem, to people who were neither, to some extent both.

"So you've decided to come over, Angel?"

"Sort of, Mommy. I've called you with an Art Problem." Gill lent this statement full importance by pausing to adjust his glasses. "You can't interrupt me because it's important. It's not about the investments—those are on the way to Rupert. It's more a . . . well . . ."

"Anouk's. Yes, Alain said so. Still here, darling. Isabelle has popped by."

"I think it may be a spiritual crisis."

"Oh?"

Gill held the receiver very close and gazed intently into the middle distance. "It's been an *incredible* week."

"For me too, love. The weather has been *fabulous*."

"I haven't abandoned any principles, but I have made a significant breakthrough in my understanding of Late Modernist ethos. I'm all for Abstraction now."

"Good."

"I know. While I'll always love social realism, its earthiness, the folksy way it has and the stories it tells, I'm starting to appreciate its—"

"—do look for my red shoes."

Gill stopped talking.

"Damn. Sorry, darling. Continue. I'm all ears. I was just

**136**

wondering, though, if you can see the red Charles Jourdan slingbacks in my closet. I was sure I'd packed them."

Gill did not look. "Yes. They're right here."

"Thank you. How did this happen?"

"I've been doing a *lot* of new reading."

"Mmm."

"But actually I think James has shown me the dark side of the movement."

"Your friend. Does that lovely young man *steal*?"

"No."

"Though one wouldn't be able to tell with the house as it is."

"He's been showing me bad art with good intentions."

"Good. He was too well-mannered. I notice these things. I like James."

"I like James, too. I didn't say I didn't *like* him."

"Dearest mine, you like *everybody*."

"I like him, but he's not very *real*. Real artists are always, you know, stirring things up."

"I do indeed."

"You were an artist's model once."

"I was," she replied. "They are and we did."

"Anyway . . ." Gill looked at his picture book. "I've been reading about the Abstract Expressionists. New York School as well as the Hot New ones. I'm drawn to them."

"Ahh," Mrs. Brix-Webber said, and Gill knew he had caught her midpuff." She exhaled. "Betty Parsons is dead, which is a shame."

Gill prepared to say more about the expressionists.

"Tell me about James, Angel. I liked him so. We spoke before I left. Anyone who quotes Tolstoy on Art to me is not simple. Does he bore you?"

"He watches too much television."

"Well."

"He never goes out. He has no friends in the city. He knows next to nothing about Art. He says, 'I don't know much about Art, but I know what I like.' "

"I bet you're fibbing with that last bit."

"Well, you know what—"

"Isn't it a duty to educate people of that sort, darling? As you've said so many times, Art for the Masses and all that?"

Gill knew when he was being baited.

"Mother, I wasn't going to tell you this but he keeps a small plastic bag on the bottom of the refrigerator. Peanut butter, old apples, crumbly stacks of Ritz crackers. He has no interest in revolution or social art movements. He thinks Art is a club you can join. He thinks I want to play Swinburne to his Watts-Dunton, and he wants to do it on a budget. I can't do much with that."

A moment of transatlantic static.

"Ritz *crackers*?" After a long pause Mrs. Brix-Webber said, "I *won't* have them in my house. I won't."

"I think I've done with social realism anyway. Did I tell you I've quit the soup kitchen?"

"Darling, you're full of surprises."

"Yes, I am."

"Have you been going through galleries for Mommy?"

"No. I'm writing a novel."

Gill stood and flipped through the channels on the cable box.

"*Zut*. Extraordinary child."

The front door opened, then shut. Gill could not tell if his mother had meant it.

"I'm not a child. . . . There's nothing very good about the drawings."

"Darling."

"Yesterday he showed me one of a hot dog stand. Why would anyone draw a hot dog stand?"

"Perhaps it stood still. . . . have you told him you're leaving soon? What if he should die of malnutrition? Anyway, I meant to call—your father's coming back on business this week. You'll have to hide him or get rid of him."

"I can't just tell him to go."

"Do, darling. For Mommy's sake. You know how your father feels about artists in the house. Besides, I let something slip the other night and he's been on a rampage all week. There's no telling *what* can happen to poor James. Hurry over—bring your novel, if you like. The weather is very nice and all your friends have been asking for you."

"Right."

"Good-bye, *mon chou*. You have been warned. Kisses to you and Peanut."

"And Rupert," Gill said. "I'm seeing *Rupert* tonight."

"Rupert too. Bye-bye."

"Bye-bye," Gill said.

James had had a rough day, and by the expression on Gill's face as he walked around the corner toward his room, it would get even rougher before it got done. He had spent the first part of his day on Twelfth Avenue at 137th Street, drawing the cast-iron viaduct and the wholesale meat market. It was an uncomfortable and dirty place and his two best drawings had been ruined by pigeons just as he had been putting them into his portfolio. Then he had run out of fixative and all his other drawings had smudged. On Broadway he had watched a mother beat her child. Later a crazy person had yelled at him for five blocks before stopping into a bar. When he finally sat down at the 81st Street entrance to Central Park, people had looked at his plastic bags and his dirty hands and, he felt sure, hardened their faces and quickened their strides. Some wit had even thrown change in his knapsack.

He wanted to shower and he wanted to sleep. He did not really want to talk to Gill but hoped this did not show.

Gill seemed exceptionally ill at ease in his vague, cool, knowing way. James kept catching sight of him, eyes enormous behind gold spectacles, lips slightly pursed, almost— but not quite—managing to say something.

"Hi, Gill."

"Hello. Did you have a good day?"

"Not really." James set his plastic bags in a corner. "I think it might be the moon. People are getting pretty awful out there. I could use a break from this routine."

Gill raised his eyebrows. "I can certainly understand *that*."

"I mean," said James, "I walk around all day, just looking at things, and I don't know anybody, and nobody ever talks to me. I don't have anything particular to do. Sometimes I start wondering if I'm really alive, because nobody looks at me or notices I'm there like today unless it's some crazy person having a fit. And I drift around so much I feel like I *am* going crazy. I've started talking to myself, you know. Right in the middle of the street I'll say, 'That's okay, really,' or 'Sure . . . sure I'm sure,' or, like today, 'Okey-dokey.' " He looked hard at Gill. "Can you imagine walking around all day not knowing why you're saying, 'Okey-dokey?' I mean, I think I *am* losing it. And I'm pretty lost about my work. . . . I wish I had Dick Merisi here. Did you ever know Dick?"

"In a way."

"Well, I just wish . . ." For a moment James lost his concentration. "Last week there were three days when all I said from the moment I woke up till five in the afternoon was, 'Excuse me,' 'One, please,' and 'Hello.' And you know what?"

Gill raised his eyebrows.

"I said the 'Hello' to your doorman."

James bent and picked up his plastic bags again and began walking slowly away. "It's not your fault, Gill, really. I respect this idea you have about social realism and all. But I just think I might have to—well—"

"What?"

James, who had hoped that Gill would follow him to his room as they talked, turned around and put the bags back on the floor. "I've been thinking I need an environment," He said slowly. "A studio, that is. I need to work in a studio to make my etchings. I've got all the drawings I need. Now I need a studio, and I don't want to use the studio at the Art Students' League. *That* studio is a mess."

"Really?"

"I might have to go back to Amherst. For the *studio*, you understand."

They looked carefully at each other.

After a moment Gill pushed his glasses very deliberately up the bridge of his nose. Then he ran his hand deeply through his hair and looked down the hall at nothing in particular. He looked very disappointed.

"I think," he said slowly, "that you must do what's best for your Art. That's what's *most* important. But we'll talk about the details later." Then he brightened. "Would you like to go out this evening?"

"Gee, Gill—"

"I'm meeting Rupert Boynton. But we might also celebrate your . . . er, change of plans. Besides, we don't know how soon you might be leaving."

"In that case," James said slowly. "It might be nice. It might be a very nice send-off."

During a long, hot shower, James made several decisions. His first was to spend money. He still had $437.28 left and at Amherst he would be able to work in the dishroom again, which meant that meals would be free and he would have pocket money. Housing on campus would be cheap and he had already bought all his printmaking supplies. He could afford to humor Gill this evening and was curious, as well, about how it felt to spend money. He suspected it would make him feel powerful and really at ease. Already he was enjoying the idea.

He also decided to try, as best he could, to look carefully about himself that night at the trendy New York Art Scene that he had heard so much about, but had as yet not managed to penetrate. He thought of Marina, and wondered if he would at last see her at wherever it was they were going. He thought with trepidation of the many beautiful women he had seen in art galleries, and of high style, and of Contemporary Art in general, which he did not feel he understood but which he had, in fact, taken a very thorough course in at Smith the previous semester. (He had been intimidated by the women in that class as well.)

Preparations for the big evening were simple. James dined off peanut butter and apples in his room, accompanying his dinner with a largish pot of cold instant coffee, so that he would not get tired too early, which was a problem he had. He changed into his best, trendiest clothes, a patterned shirt and cuffed trousers, both only slightly wrinkled (he had thoughtfully hung them in the bathroom while he took his shower.) He slicked his hair back slightly with some stuff from the guest room medicine cabinet. As a final flourish of drop-dead style, James took from his Hefty bag full of clothes the shoes he had purchased with Joan that brilliant day four and a half months ago. He had not worn them all summer. He hummed to himself while dressing and wrote Joan a postcard as he waited for the evening to begin.

When they met in the hall later that night Gill took in his friend's new look with the usual expression of distanced amusement and concern. James noticed this, as well as his friend's new outfit: an old tropical-weight khaki suit with a short tie and brown wing tips. Gill explained this was the Franz Kline Look so recently taken up by the Hot New Abstract Expressionists featured in the *Sunday Times Magazine* and *Vogue*. Peanut, he hastened to add, would accompany them. Rupert loved Peanut.

The elevator arrived; they descended, all three quiet before the doorman. A cab awaited outside.

"Tabac, please," Gill said. And settling back with Peanut in the middle, they spoke more of Art, and of Gill's recent interest in Hot New Abstract Expressionism.

The Cafe Tabac, internationally renowned watering hole of the New York art world, had been in Mrs. Brix-Webber's more social days her favorite stomping ground, a home away from home on the downtown gallery scene. She knew everyone and everything there, every artist and gallery person, consequently about every show, sale, and scandal. Gill had been there with her in his Dalton years, during that time managing to observe a vast procession of artists, agents, owners, as well as the rich, the powerful, the glamorous—all, in fact, who kept in touch with The Happening New York Art Scene. Since Art and Fashion and Theater Scenes had much in common, he had known just about everyone who was anyone anywhere, either as they were becoming or just as they became, and he had met them at the Tabac—which, worldwide reputation aside, was a very comfortable place to meet and mingle with the known world and its invited guests, especially if, like the Brix-Webbers, one owned shares in the place and drank at half-price.

Gill had explained something of the Tabac to James on the way down, but evidently not enough. The flashing lights, the lines stretching around the block, the liveried doormen in their high patent-leather boots, as well as the jugglers, fire-eaters, and ragged little girls selling cellophane-wrapped roses outside the doors (as limousine after limousine swept through a sea of yellow cabs toward the impossibly crowded, floodlit entrance) were all somewhat surprising to one who had spent his summer mostly uptown.

"We'll never get in here," James said.

"Get serious."

Calling to a large man at the door and flashing a small lavender card, as well as Peanut (hoisted aloft on the card-waving arm), Gill secured their entry through a sea of similarly dressed people crowded around, begging, muttering, cursing, and waving twenty-dollar bills.

They made their way inside. Overhead, quotes by famous artists (*"Il n'y a pas de solution parce qu'il n'y pas de problème"* being James' favorite) lit the ceiling in sculpted neon; on raised platforms, models composed *tableaux vivants* of blue-period harlequins, party-colored card players, or nudes in deck chairs and on hammocks. A woman dressed in shingles walked up and down steps.

They headed inward and downward past fountains and lasers to a central area cordoned off from the general public but plainly visible through a shield of bullet-proof glass. Peanut now walked by himself and seemed right at home.

"Welcome to the *hub*," Gill said.

Gill said hello to a friend at the door, and they were granted entry. *Hub* was right; the plan of the place was circular, sunken toward the bar at the middle. Sitting in any of the several tiers in the room one had a clear view of all that was going on; it was rather like a dimly lit colosseum or senate chamber done up in a pink with chrome trim. The rings descended at increasingly smaller intervals, finding their focus in the iced cocktail glasses resting on the bar at center. The room was very crowded, but hushed, and waiters and waitresses passed busily to and fro with the aloof, knowing expressions of down-at-the-heels members of the social register.

None of the clientele were anywhere near as impressive as the waiting staff or decor. Most, in fact, looked like bankers, lawyers, and saleswomen, and many had tucked their briefcases between their legs in preference to checking them outside. A few clothes designers added local color; occasionally design school types, dressed in leopard-skin pants, turbans, and sunglasses, passed down to the bar at center, only to look around coolly and wander out again. The place looked rather less exciting than the other rooms outside, at least to James. But as there had been so many people outside trying so hard to get in, and there were so many others pressing their noses against the tinted glass even as James sat down, almost everyone inside, he noticed, was scanning the room with interest, as if somewhere nearby lurked the answer to an age-old riddle or a prize for individual beauty or merit. No one looked particularly happy. James noted immediately that the drinks were very expensive.

"Do artists really come here?"

Gill shrugged.

"Those who can. Those who can't wish they could. This is the place they Make Connections."

"Are any here now? Me not included, of course."

Gill smiled and began to point them out.

James had studied almost all of the vast and assorted array of artists in his modern art course at Smith. Old Pops and Ops, the ex-wife of a dead Expressionist, two Post-Expressionists, a Conceptualist sitting with a tired Super-Realist, and a few of the early Post-Modernists standing up near the door; all well-dressed and well-mannered, all gazing about with the bored, abstracted gaze of success. As it was a warmish night several drank colorful fruit slush drinks, some garnished with paper umbrellas, oranges, and maraschino cherries. None behaved particularly controversially or looked particularly interesting; none were especially conversational; most, as perhaps befits the visual artist, appeared more engaged in observation than discussion. German electronic music played; a noted minimalist ate chef's salad.

"I'm buying tonight," James said.

"Impossible," Gill replied, "Everything here is on account. Besides, you couldn't afford it."

"I *want* to buy."

"But you can't," Gill said. "That's all there is to it. Now," he looked around, "who can I point out to you? Those are two of the top gallery owners in the city. They're friends of my family. And that's Rupert Boynton on the far left. He's sitting with Todd Wolff, the designer."

James looked but did not see whom Gill had pointed out.

"Boynton? Of Boynton-Crest? Wow. Where?"

"Let me introduce you."

Rupert Boynton of Boynton-Crest International, the most infamous and highly renowned of fast-track contemporary art dealers, had long existed in James' imagination as the *Tyrannosaurus rex* of the dark, steamy, savagely antagonistic New York Art World described in ladies' magazines and popular fiction. His ability to make or break the career of any contemporary artist had long been impressed upon James by Gill, who had grown up with his children and watched "The Brady Bunch" in his home on Beekman Place. His reputation for ruthless manipulation and occasional double-dealing had brought to mind the tight-lipped, small-eyed, surly counte-nanced man who sat far across the room by himself, looking very important; obviously all semblance of Christian virtue had long ago been wrung, ounce by ounce, from his thick, gnomish body. James could not spot his companion at all.

"Is that him?"

"No, don't be silly," Gill said. "He's there sitting with Todd Wolff."

They crossed the room. Before reaching their destination, however, James was stopped cold by a face looming from the dim crowd clustered at the bar. Dark and swarthy, it baffled him with its familiarity until the crowd parted and they stood face-to-face. Then James recognized him immediately; it was the Hot New Abstract Expressionist featured in the *Times Magazine* and celebrated loud and long by Joan: Sancho. She had long ago pointed out that he dared wear black tie in midafternoon. Apparently he wore it at night as well. James asked for an autograph but the artist declined with a heavy accent. "For business reasons," Gill whispered as they con-tinued on toward Mr. Boynton's table. "Never ask an artist to sign *any*thing."

They stopped for a moment by a somewhat short, broad, smiling businessman with an extraordinarily smooth pinkish complexion, speaking with animation to a short dark man. His fair hair had thinned almost to nothing atop his shiny head, and his round face gave the impression of not so much a middle-aged man as a fat chuckling baby, smiling with wet lips as he rolled his enormous, unfocused blue eyes. His suit was pale gray, of a European cut, and his pale yellow tie was held in place by a large sapphire set in platinum. Like a tot on his first day at school, he held his round hands clasped gently and reverently together on the table before him.

They were perhaps the most strikingly beautiful hands that James had ever seen. Perfectly white, hairless, of a soft, even texture, proportioned so that each plump finger (two wearing plain gold bands, the rest conspicuously bare) tapered uniformly down to a blunt rounded end. The nails, however, were what really amazed: perfectly smooth and exquisitely shaped, even and glossy and surrounded by flawless cuticles. Each baby-pink oblong displayed at its base, like priceless treasures incomparably matched with nine others of the same startling and marvelous hue, a delicate pale white crescent moon.

"Rupert," Gill said. "Rupert Boynton."

The man looked up, smiling.

"Gill," he said, "my dear young friend. And Peanut— and—so good to see you all."

He rose and smiled broadly, revealing a plenitude of tiny white teeth and one gold filling. He spoke with a slight English accent. They embraced.

"And how is Oriane?" he asked, referring to Mrs. Brix-Webber. Gill told them she was fine and introduced James. Boynton's companion, Mr. Wolff, introduced himself as "Todd" and then Mr. Boynton asked them to sit, signaling the waitress.

"Demitasse all around, Verena."

The coffee arrived almost before they could speak, black and steaming in tiny little cups with tiny little spoons and tiny curved slices of glistening lemon zest. Gill and Mr. Boynton and Mr. Wolff chattered happily, sipping coffee. James watched, amazed, as the large ruddy man, sitting up very straight in his chair, took the pale cup and saucer to his chest; from there the cup continued up to his lips, returning shortly thereafter to the tiny saucer poised over the large smooth hand. The exquisite beringed finger held the tiny cup with the greatest delicacy, like the most fragile work of art, and throughout the ensuing conversation James could not take his eyes from them.

After a few courteous inquiries Boynton said to Gill, "You know, we've bought all the paintings of that man you recommended to us."

He smiled broadly, once again flashing his brilliant tiny teeth from behind finely shaped wet lips. Gill looked at him with upraised eyebrows.

"For an opening this fall—you must excuse us if we talk business a moment, James—at a flat rate. Two thousand percent profit. I've got the work already. I bought his wife out quite, *quite* reasonably, you know. We've found something here, something marvelous. How can I thank you? You'll receive your agent's fee on it, of course. Enough to buy a small home in the country with, I suspect."

"Marvelous," Gill said somewhat tentatively, flashing a quick look toward James, who was still watching Mr. Boynton, fascinated. "Rupert, that's wonderful."

"At first we wouldn't consider it. The paintings are fine . . . that is, not extraordinary but strong enough so that with the proper buildup they'll do very well. They've got that tortured private life going for them . . . that *atmosphere*."

He looked from Gill to James, his bright eyes wide with delight as he contemplated the success of his deal, focusing at last with a momentary intensity on James' interested face.

"You see, the artist took his own life—not an unheard-of thing by any means, except that it happened at the most wonderfully privileged place, and a number of pictures happened to have been taken by the college photographer—something of an artist himself, if these pictures are any indication. And then the coroner's report and a few of the documents left behind make it all very marketable. . . . It won't do the poor bugger very well, will it, but it will make him famous and I suppose that's the most he could want." He turned to Gill. "I think I may get *People* to cover it. That means phone calls from Oklahoma."

James looked at Gill. His expression had quickly gone from fascination to confusion to blank horror. He was very pale, and Mr. Wolff later noted his mouth hung open in a most unattractive way. Boynton continued.

"Hel-lo, Peanut. Wonderful dog you have." Then, "We're working on the biographical bits right how. It *will* cause a stir. We may get a lead in the *Times Arts and Leisure* if we make it—how does one say it?" Mr. Boynton looked carefully round the table. "—a 'real sob story,' isn't that right?"

"Fabulous possibilities," Mr. Wolff said, nodding agreement. "I may take the T-shirt concession."

"You had Monaco up at Amherst. That prince," Boynton said, wiggling his eyebrows at James. "That's the sort of thing that sells in Texas. Rather like *gold*, you know—and was there a child of the Shah as well? I must check. So many of our Iranian expatriates buy art and they might be especially interested to know our man taught royalty. They have a great eye for quality, you know. All Easterners do."

Gill broke in rather tentatively. "James studied under him, you know."

"The Shah?" Rupert asked, delighted.

James looked at Gill. "Merisi," he said.

"How wonderful." He looked at Gill. "Did you know him at the time of the suicide?"

James nodded.

"Ever hint at anything to you about it?"

"Well," he said slowly, "he sent me a note, but it was Xeroxed. Gill, you never told me about *any* of this."

"Oh, yes. There were several copies of that. We've seen *that*." Boynton rattled on, somewhat apologetically adding, "It's of crucial importance to the catalogue, of course. But you wouldn't happen to know the real story, would you? Who or what in particular drove him to it? A love interest, perhaps? Love gone wrong? Desperate over some cold-hearted debutante?"

"He was very shy." He turned to Gill. "You are a horrible person."

"Horrible?" Mr. Boynton asked. "Horrible?"

"Of course I'm not. But you're not the only person making his way in the art world. Let's talk about this later."

"Hmm . . . yes, well, we might work some bit of that in once it's all sorted out. Come down for the opening, James. I'll give Gill an invitation for you. It's been so nice to meet you." He looked around. "But must you be going?"

Gill rose, blushing.

"I'm sorry, Rupert," Gill said, "We really must be going."

James rose, glaring from one to the other.

"Not really?" Boynton said.

"Yes."

"If you must. Please stop by soon. We'd love seeing you again."

"Yes, we may. Thank you."

"I won't."

Boynton and Wolff remained seated; Gill shook hands with them. James stood off to one side, awkward and furious. Gill promised to give Boynton's regards to Oriane. Just before they left something occurred to him.

"How about the other?" he asked. "That portfolio I brought down from Amherst? Concerning shoes. Frank Mathews?"

Mr. Boynton shook his head.

"Well, thanks once more."

"Not at all, dear boy."

The rest of the evening passed uneventfully. After a few hostile remarks by James Gill did not talk. Eventually he wandered off by himself and met some friends. James wandered out of the room to the rest of the club, and looked around for people he knew, and when he didn't recognize anyone he began to feel silly. Just as he was about to leave he met Gill again.

"I'm leaving."

"So am I."

In the taxi home Gill asked James what his plans were. James suggested he might leave the next morning.

"I have to, actually. I'd like to get back to work. It's a question of facilities."

"Do you have to?"

"I have to."

"Well, if you have to, you have to."

This time James paid for the cab. He gave the man a twenty and took no change, but the man didn't even say thank you and it only made him feel like more of a chump.

That night, wired on demitasse, he sat up until dawn, packing his drawings, cleaning up his journal, then lying on the bed and staring at the patchy, rust-stained ceiling, which still could be heard dropping plaster throughout the large silent house. When he finally did nod off somewhere near six, he dreamt of the artists at the Tabac, yawning, staring, sitting in place, contentedly picking the cherries from their iced fruit drinks.

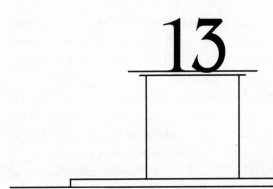

# 13

Rather than go straight back to Amherst, he decided to take a last class at the League, then return to his mother's to pick up the spare clothes and drawings he had left when he moved to Gill's. He suspected he would stay the weekend with her. No one at Amherst would expect him until Monday and he had, as yet, no place to stay. Leaving the Brix-Webbers' was altogether more simple. Gill had slept in. James looked at the books a bit more, wandered through the rooms of dusty collectibles, and left a little before noon without saying good-bye to his host. Instead he left a note with a promise to call soon and the portrait he had done.

The young man had a great deal to think about on his walk to the League and a great deal to carry as well. All of his things had packed neatly into two plastic bags and a portfolio; rather than take the crowded bus down Fifth and another across Fifty-seventh Street, he opted for the more direct route through the park, soon realizing he had vastly underestimated the weight of his luggage. A heat wave had struck; the benches were empty of the people he had hoped to stop and draw; everyone else looked vaguely bothered and self-important. There was nothing at all pleasant about the day. He had been drinking too much coffee for much too long; in combination with the heat and lack of sleep, it made him feel nervous, exhausted, and moody.

At Columbus Circle, amid lunch-hour traffic, he looked up at a bus moving slowly down Broadway and in the framed grouping of torsos and heads thought he recognized his old friend Marina. It may not have been her. She was wearing a large number of metal objects like fish hooks and safety pins in her ear, and had cut off most of her hair. Though he ran for a short distance beside the bus he was unable to capture her attention. He looked silly with his Hefty bags anyway.

Before class, he sat once more in the lobby with the shopping bag lady, whose name was Etta. As he turned through the pages of his pad she said, "No, honey. You'll never be an artist like that. That's awful."

But then she offered him a cigarette, which he took though he did not smoke: he was grateful for, and ready to accept, any token of consolation.

Class dragged on forever. Gloria had not come, nor any of the other familiar models. There had been some sort of last-minute emergency, so that when a model finally was secured, he turned out to be a very old, greasy-haired derelict who wore a small black snood to mask his privates. He smelled so bad that most of the students either drew from the far corner of the room or left. James thought it by far the most depressing moment of the summer.

Somewhere around four he tapped George and lifted a hand

in farewell. He waved to Henry, who did not look up from his work. The wino stared and the students drew. James closed the door softly and, in doing so, briefly entertained the idea they would never leave.

In the lobby he stopped over by Etta.

"Hi, honey."

"Hi, Etta. Look, can you watch these bags for me? There's a fiver in it for you if you take good care of 'em."

"Sure, honey. Just leave 'em with me."

"Thanks. I'll be back around seven."

"I ain't goin' nowhere, honey. I got the steps out front tonight."

He decided to go to the park until rush hour was over; he did not want to risk crushing his art on the subway.

He went back to Columbus Circle to draw carriage horses. It was harder than he thought it would be. Sitting on a bench, surrounded by traffic and people, he managed several good compositions and few interesting studies of the horses them-selves, but people everywhere were hurrying and nasty and the loud congested traffic filled the area with thick heavy fumes.

After one more drawing James began to feel like he couldn't breathe. He rose and walked back into the park, where he bought a Coke and sat at a shaded picnic table for quite a while. The shade was very pleasant. His dizziness passed. Across the playing field a softball game was going on. He wrote in his journal, looked at the trees, and then eventually wandered over to watch the game.

Both the softball teams were immaculately dressed in full outfits, trousers and jerseys and gaiters, with the team names emblazoned on the shirts and an insignia set into the caps in bright crisp colors. People were jumping up and down on the sidelines, cheering their teams and drinking beer.

"I really need a new pair of sneakers," James said. He was talking to himself.

They were corporate teams. A prestigious bank was playing a top-flight ad agency. Someone seemed to be waving him off the field, which was strange, because looking down, he saw he was nowhere near the baseline.

The person continued to wave. It was Stubby. Carol stood beside him. Carol said something, smiling, that James could not hear.

"Hi!"

"Hi."

Stubby and Carol were working for the bank and had decided to come to the game even though they were not on the teams, really. At the end of last semester they had all agreed to get together in the city. Now they had.

The banking was going well. Living in New York was very exciting.

"We've been doing just about everything," Carol said. James explained he would soon return to Amherst. After a while James said he had to be getting home.

"Good-bye," they said.

" 'Bye."

But he did not go home. He decided to go to the movies instead, relatively sure that his mother would not arrive home until late. After getting no answer when he called, he stopped back by the League for his bags.

"You back fast, baby," Etta said.

"Yeah. Here's your five, Etta. I appreciate it."

"No problem."

"I'll send you a postcard here from Massachussetts."

"Okay, honey."

Then he brought all of his things up to the Regency for the

late double feature. By the time he left it was near midnight and relatively quiet for Broadway at that hour. He caught the IRT local at Seventy-second Street, and by some strange miracle got a seat in an air-conditioned car. The car filled quickly. Taking out an anatomy book, he looked again at the various reproductions of great art: Proudhon, Egon Schiele, Michelangelo, Oskar Kokoschka.

Gradually James became aware that the man beside him was leaning over to look at the pictures as well. He was humming a Luther Vandross song that Mrs. Sloan liked to do her aerobics to called "Busy Bee," and his breath smelled heavily of Juicy Fruit gum.

James looked at him. He wore white tube socks, high-top sneakers, and a knotted piece of nylon stocking on his head. He looked very tough.

The subway rose onto the El. The tension in the car seemed to relax a bit; the roaring of the train diminished in open air, and, crawling along slowly on the high trestle above 125th Street, there was suddenly a leisurely, day-trippy feeling to the ride. A lot of people got off at the 125th Street stop.

"You do art?"

James nodded, looking carefully at the person beside him. Late twenties; sweatband; Fu Manchu mustache, large jaw, chipped teeth.

"I like art." He tapped the pad on the floor between them. "Can I see?"

James showed him a series of drawings done of people waiting on line at a bank. He seemed to like them.

"Do one of me."

"How far are you going?"

"137th."

"We're almost there."

"I'll stay on."

James considered. "Okay."

The train went back underground. Picking up speed, it seemed once again in a hurry to arrive somewhere, once more full of sweaty, impatient people. At 137th, James said, "Let's get off here. I'll catch the next train."

The man nodded.

James was somewhat impressed to find himself on an empty IRT platform in Harlem after midnight, drawing. He did not know why he was doing it. They sat on a bench some ways down from the change booth. As James drew his model told his life story. He was a backup singer. He was on his way to visit his mother. There were different backup singers, he explained, some for studio work and some for performing. He was a studio backup singer. He had grown up on Tremont Avenue. "I am Amad Jamahl," he concluded. "Let me see the picture."

James showed him the drawing, not knowing what to expect.

The man's expression did not change. "How much you want for it?"

James thought about it. "I don't think I really want to sell it."

"I give you three bucks."

"Three?"

"Three bucks."

James stared up at the ceiling for a moment. What the hell. "Okay."

Amad looked surprised. "Lemme get change."

He disappeared toward the change booth and did not come back for some time. James put the drawing in his bag and walked up to the booth. There was no one there and the man inside was asleep. He got on the next train with the drawing, which was not very good, and arrived home about an hour later.

"So you're back," Mrs. Sloan said. "I have to say I expected as much. You were never a very polite houseguest, even as a very small child. I suppose you left wet towels on the floor at your friend's house, too."

She said this through the door. After a prolonged fidgeting with three new locks, the door opened two inches to reveal half of Mrs. Sloan's face and a brand-new police chain.

"Luckily I saw you from the window. But, dear heart, please call before you come home next time. For all you knew, I might have been in Paris—or had a *houseguest* of my own."

She closed the door to open it.

Mrs. Sloan looked well. She seemed to have lost weight in the past two weeks, and was wearing a new silk nighty and an emerald-green robe. Her last words had been uttered with such intentional significance that James could not help asking, as he seated himself on the sofa, who that particular houseguest might be.

"Well, I don't suppose I can keep anything from you for very long," Mrs. Sloan said, quite concernedly. "I've met someone I like very much. I hope you will, too. But if you don't it won't make any difference. The best thing is, he works down the hall from me."

"Mom, that's great."

"*I* think so. He's much better looking than your father. . . . Do you feel all right?"

"Me? Fine."

"You don't look well at all. I've noticed that you don't stand up straight since you became an artist."

"It's been a long day."

"Have you become an artist?"

"I don't think anymore than the last time we spoke."

"Good. Maybe your posture won't get any worse, then. I've been worrying about your posture. It's been terrible all summer. I didn't want to say anything, of course, because as an artist you had such terrible fits of temperament. But now that that phase is behind you perhaps you'll sit up that much taller in your seat."

"And how have you been these past weeks?"

"Don't change the subject." She smiled blankly. "You know, I did go to Madrid briefly. I stay at the Ritz there. It's very nice. I have some Ritz notepaper if you want it. . . . I was hoping you'd come feed the cat. He had to go a little hungry instead, though. I don't suppose you received my message?"

"I did," James said. "Mom, we *talked*. You didn't say anything about Madrid."

She looked up, eyebrows twitching slightly. "Oh . . . my mistake. Would you like a Tab?"

"No thanks."

"I've stopped drinking diet cola. I want those ones you bought out of the refrigerator. Be sure to drink them before you leave."

"I'll see what I can do."

"Help yourself to lime as well. How long are you staying?"

"I thought I'd stay the weekend."

"Hmm. Well, darling, I'm hardly about to kick you out. Heaven knows I'm not the sort of mother who throws her son out on the street—"

"—I know."

"—Especially since he's mended his ways. But I've actually already made plans. You'll have to clear out by Saturday. A friend of yours has been calling for the past few days. A girl named Joan. She's been remarkably unpleasant. Is she attractive? It's so hard to tell over the phone."

"She's okay. Did she leave a number?"

"No. A message."

Mrs. Sloan rose from her seat and headed into the kitchen. "Here you are," she called. "It says, 'Moving in this weekend.' I wonder if *you* could move in, too, wherever that is."

"I will, Mom," James said. "Go to hell."

"Attaboy," Mrs. Sloan said from the kitchen. "You're sure you wouldn't like a Tab?"

# Epilogue

Lillian Gilder thought that during spring rains, no building at Amherst stood out with such remarkable beauty as the red-brick palazzo she worked in, known until so recently as the fine arts building. Under a flat purple-gray sky, the tender greens and pinks of young plants surrounding it stood rooted in place by the intense, earthy color of the building itself, bright wet red, outlined in black above and below by glistening slate and glistening asphalt. The place had a luminous, unearthly presence—or rather, she liked to think, the earthly presence of all that might have been, for the promise it held under rain seemed not of this world.

Walking before it now with her old black umbrella to survey the flowerbeds soon to be hers no longer, she thought how she had envisioned, financed, and planted those flowers herself, no help from the college. She remembered the trip to the greenhouses, the buying of mosses, bulbs, and seeds;

remembered kneeling with trowels on a raw, windy Saturday just a few years ago. Now, standing beside them, she knew the futility of her endeavor, knew that despite all her insistent attempts, the department would never dwell in a collegiate garden of earthly delights: professors and students and flowering plants would never come together in and around this old building, practicing art in Pre-Raphaelite tranquillity; nor would she, Vermeer-like, sit quietly by the high, wide windows reading letters, writing memos, or balancing accounts for the petty cash box. The whole lot of them—students, professors, and departmental secretary alike—were bound for a place altogether more appropriate to art in the modern age. Word was out: Fine Arts was going underground, to dusty obscurity and life entombment, and Lillian, because it was her job, would be going, too.

"Change *was* necessary," she said aloud to herself.

Perhaps the ad hoc report had been right; the present department was a few sullen professors endlessly quoting Ruskin, its program a halfhearted tip-o'-the-hat to culture, promoting nothing so much as supervised hobbies and Saturday cocktails. Perhaps they did lag a full century behind their contemporaries and despite all good intentions did absolutely nothing to help students prepare for the Real World of Art—that sort of talk made her feel old and slightly ridiculous. That was not *her* art department; that had no bearing on the so many wonderful things that had happened in this building, practically before her eyes. No, she would not consider it. She put it from her mind.

Shaking her umbrella under the arcade, she thought of the word arcade: *Et in Arcadia Ego,* a painting by Poussin. Lovely paintings, yes; but the flowers she had bought, planted, and tended would never be hers; students like those she had known would not come again; only the tenured professors were dug in for good. There would be no more gardening. Not where she was going.

She climbed the steps to her office, slowly, deliberately, feeling her feet fit the half-moons worn into stone, and in them the most reassuring sense of placement, of reason, of security. Art is not what it once was, she thought; students of art are not, either; no one behaves as he should. She would sauna that afternoon, later bake cookies; then she would feel better.

The stairs made her breathless sometimes, now, with rain, they made her knees hurt as well. She stood a moment at the head of the stairs. The stairs would be shorter in the new place, down instead of up; perhaps it was better to move if only for that reason. She sighed, unlocked her door, and dropped her umbrella into her stand with a solid, reassuring clunk.

She could still hardly believe they were being evicted. But quiet investigations into Merisi's death had fortuitously concluded just as wide-scale changes in the student social life had been implemented. The administration, in its reevaluation of the department, had decided quite arbitrarily that it might also move; as a small disreputable group with several members on leave and fewer students each year, it had little claim to the spacious building it called home.

The switch had been quietly, easily, heartlessly effected, and the new plans for the building had just recently been announced. The beautiful old building would be gutted for a social center, its solid antique furnishings ripped out for plasterboard walls, its oak floors left, beer-sticky, to furnish the bleak dark rooms of dispirited keg parties. The fine arts department, for its part, would wander for a year to a building across campus (poorly insulated, lit by fluorescent tubes) and from there, in time, move again, this time out of sight, underground, to a bunker under the art museum where, with adequate funding and inadequate lighting, untouched by morning and untouched by noon, the tiny department would slowly subside into dust.

Lillian knew that without the pleasant situation of its offices the program would collapse, but saw no use complaining. The decision had been final, and everyone, department and administration alike, knew the implications of the decision, and nonetheless moved on to other more pressing concerns. Pike and Williams were lying low, while the rest of the department was either on leave or not on speaking terms with those whose decisions they might contest. No one was really to blame, thought Lillian, yet it seemed a great pity that the days of happy commitment and sunny contemplation, of well-dressed young curator-types tending the gallery, bohemians in paint-stained jeans standing by with coffee, should all now end. But they would, for without the stylish visibility of students assuming their role as guardians of culture, without a snack bar hard by dispensing vision, ambition, and a certain necessary *gemütlichkeit,* the program was to a certain extent doomed. Who would venture to a bleak hole below the ugly museum where four sulky professors huddled warily about an expiring Mr. Coffee? One or two of strong stomach and weak judgment, perhaps; the rest would take courses at Smith and that would be that.

Lillian went to her desk and read her calendar for the day. She had little to do besides send out bulletins announcing the bus trips to New York and the Wadsworth Athenaeum. There would of course be Professor Pike's appointments to arrange and his advisees to placate, but that was routine, and moreover something she liked; daily remonstration kept larger issues safely at a distance. Lydia would certainly stop over for coffee.

There was a committee meeting to discuss the visiting artists for the next semester; she had bought cider and apples, and picked flowers as well. There wasn't much more to do.

An oaktag folder sat on her desk: a sheaf of articles on Dick Merisi's posthumous opening in New York. His work had gone over big. She was pleased to think she had known him. But the phone calls were a trial; recently *American Artist*, *ArtNews*, and even *Art in America* had tried to make her talk about the suicide. Of course she had given away nothing. She didn't gossip, didn't want trouble; didn't want Pike or Williams to have any more to think about than they already did. She had witnessed the hesitant moment between them as they read the articles through and that was enough. They had looked so terribly sorry. Besides, anything more might jeopardize the functioning of the department; the department always came first. They would not pull such a stunt again, certainly not for a while. The ad hoc committee had specifically warned them against it.

There was one more note penciled in on the bottom of the calendar.

"Of course," she said, and smiled. She knew there had been something; she had promised to advise James Sloan on the purchase of cheese. His opening was that afternoon; he would be in at any moment. She smoothed her dress before her and adjusted her reading glasses, then reached for a filebox holding the recommended cheese purchases, classified for groups of varying size and type, all written out in her neat cursive hand.

She liked James. He was a very odd student but then most of the department's majors were; she had an especial warmth for those such as him, baffled and indecisive, smart and somewhat good-looking, though his posture could be better. They were a precocious flock, these students; ever needful of compassion as they passed so timidly beneath her watchful eyes. She was generally pleased to oblige them; James, certainly.

They had become friends that August. Amid the general uproar during the deparmental investigation, he had worked steadily on in the basement print shop, oblivious and self-assured. Whenever things seemed especially rotten she would stop down to say hello.

She did not quite know why he had come back so early but thought it nicer that way; he seemed very happy and kept very busy, spending eleven or twelve hours a day in the studio. He and Joan, the actress working for buildings and grounds, made a very nice couple. She knew from her friend Carla in the dean's office that they were living together in specific violation of summer housing rules. She herself had seen them sit in the shade of the beech trees reading the *Times* on Sunday morning, and as she had been young once she approved. Moreover, though *her* opinion counted for little in the department, she thought he had done well on his fellowship, even without the supervision of Dick Merisi. He had given her a signed edition of a favorite print just before Labor Day, which now hung in her guest bathroom, framed. *A Central Park Landscape*, he called it.

Today was his opening, the last opening to be held at this building's student gallery, the small lovely room under the arcade. She thought it would be rather a good one. James had been planning it with her for months. He had carefully researched all funding, so that his extensive budget came not only from the department's gallery fund, but also from the student activities committee and the Friends of Fine Art Student Fund, with which he could legitimately purchase large quantities of alcohol. He had meticulously spackled and repainted the gallery, as well as matted or framed every drawing;

moreover he had stolen all the potted palms and geraniums from the second floor, installing them (temporarily, he had assured her) in the gallery, so that while the room had all the elegance of serious, monochromatic art it also maintained a lush garden party cheer of its own. She looked forward herself to going downstairs at the end of the day, if only for a moment. She liked going to openings on rainy days, when weather as well as art conspired to encourage late afternoon tippling. And James was handling everything in the best possible way. He was not nervous; sometimes he almost seemed not to care, though she knew he did.

She knew his footsteps and was ready when, several minutes later, dressed for the weather in an enormous tweed overcoat and fedora (which he held, dripping, before him in his hands), James peeked through the door and entered the room. He certainly was big for an artist, Lillian thought. Though impressive in bulk and dress, he wore as always his worried, sheepish expression.

"Hullo."

"Hello—Come in, come in . . . welcome."

"Thanks."

"How are you today?"

"Fine, thanks. . . . And you?"

"Fine."

"Wonderful."

"Good."

"Yes . . . not nervous?"

"Should I be?"

"Of course not . . . I just thought—"

"Mmmmm," he nodded. "No."

"Good."

"About cheese, Lillian."

"Of course."

He pulled up a chair and they spoke about cheeses. Then James stood, picked up his hat, and smiled. She knew for a fact he had capably researched the ceiling of each budget, checking each with the appropriate authorities, yet he still looked as if he felt about to do something not quite right. Though his expression lacked neither resolution nor understanding, it was without its summer resilience. He looked tired: more mature and less hopeful.

"Thank you. Good-bye."

Lillian stood as he left the office, then turned to the window to check on a slip of African violet. As she stood at the high window, her eyes wandered from furry leaf to rain splashing hard on the ledge, then below to James, setting out to cheese-shop in his big coat and hat. She switched on the radio; lately, as the office had seemed much too quiet, she had begun listening to talk shows on the local public station.

Five minutes before the opening, James stood with Joan at the center of the gallery wondering whether anyone would notice a discrepancy between the artwork and the refreshments. He certainly had. While the drawings were simple, stark renderings of urban decay, the two refreshment tables and bar looked really swank. He was rather pleased with it.

Joan stood putting the finishing touch on a basket of crackers. ". . . I wonder if Inez really will wear her hat. Do you think so? Trouble, Jamie?"

She was being attentive, in the adorable if predictable way she had when dressed up: her serious party manners.

"I was just thinking how nice you look."

She nodded, sorting through water biscuits, cream biscuits, sweetmeals, and stoned wheats, placing each type in its orderly row or semicircle. He stood still, watching her from the end of the table.

"It cost a fortune to dry-clean but this *is* the party of the century . . . definitely the place for People Worth Knowing. Too bad Gill isn't here."

James tapped his foot, preoccupied with the imminent display of curatorial prowess. He was not worried about the art. He had done a number of drawings of Joan in August that he was proud of, worked very hard at translating several of his best drawings to prints. A one-man movement had come and gone; he had long since ceased to worry about the social relevance of his work, no matter what Gill said. And as Gill was in Pakistan researching public education and going on camera safari, he had not said much in the past four months. In lieu of sending an invitation to the third world, James had sent an invitation to Mrs. Brix-Webber, one to which she had not yet replied. Remembering the piles of mail that sat unopened all about the house, he doubted she would, but that did not concern him; he would send her the review with another thank-you note soon.

That morning, a telegram had arrived for him at the campus P.O. It read:

DEAR HEART STOP IT ISNT EVERY DAY ONE CHOOSES
BETWEEN DRIVING TO AN OPENING AND ELOPING TO
THE SEYCHELLES STOP AM SO HAPPY FOR YOU STOP
YOULL SEE THE MAN AT XMAS STOP AFTER ALL IVE SEEN
THE ART STOP LOVE AND KISSES AND GO FOR IT STOP
MOM STOP

The man in the booth had been quick to point out that his mother could have used periods had she wanted to. Joan and Inez volunteered to take pictures to send to Mrs. Sloan and James had thought that a very fine and sensible suggestion. "The Seychelles are Just the Place," Inez had said when she saw the telegram. James had thought so, too. "So much for special guests," he said to Joan, who nodded, looking at the crackers with concern.

While social relevance was one thing safely out of the picture, presentation was another thing altogether, something to to be concerned about. He noted with some satisfaction the softly lit Brie, the white grapes, the Leerdammer, the small but noticeable wedge of St. André. There had been a special deal to make with the cheese merchant; by preparing the platters himself he had saved money, and by buying in bulk and cubing the end pieces of crowd-pleaser cheeses (cheddar, Muenster, Swiss) he had achieved a significant discount on over-the-counter prices, splitting the difference on dry-roasted peanuts and a can of black olives.

Joan walked to the bar she had constructed of two sculpture stands placed back to back. He knew how excited she was; how she had stood at a mirror practicing a cool, knowing, "Can I get you a drink?" late the night before. Now she looked archly at the liquor, at James, then back again.

He laughed.

"Scooter, we're *such* bad news."

"We are."

"But we should have thought it up long ago."

Several days before they had decided that the only suitable beverage at such an event would be beer. Informal, friendly, fun: Cerveza Rheingold for drawings of urban hard times. But just that afternoon it had seemed there would be no liquid refreshment at all; without a keg deposit and a tap deposit and money for the beer itself (James' own bank account was, predictably, empty), he had stood in the package store puzzled and wet in his big dripping overcoat, then wandered listlessly up and down the aisles muttering. What would he do? What *could* he do?

Then, turning the corner, it was as if divine grace had settled in a mantle of scarlet about his shoulders. Relief and delight: he had come to the end of his search. The C-and-C package store had just that day begun a once-a-decade clearance on all its jumbo-sized bottles of Johnnie Walker Red.

He had thought carefully about scotch for several minutes. It was a controversial beverage. Few drank it. But then, he drank it; Joan drank it; all their friends drank it. Among the theater clique it was greatly in vogue. Besides, there was left-over white wine in the storage closet for the gallery women. The sum total for two enormous bottles, tax included, was twenty-seven cents under his maximum budget; that had been the clincher.

"Wrap them up, please."

And now the two bottles sat before them on the sculpture stand, one for him and one for her, comprising with ice and soda and a stack of clear punch cups all the utterly complex simplicity of super-realist still life. He had told his friends to come early and now, thanks to limited amounts of this precious amber fluid, they would. Or rather, they had, for they were waiting outside.

"Looks great."

James nodded, knowing deep down that his own good lighting made it so. Under that magical lighting, arranged with such precision days before, everything—liquor, soda, plastic cups, and ice—glittered with a fierce, cold, heartless splendor.

"Five minutes, Scooter."

It would be a good opening.

People had lined up at the door, and with the clink of ice on plastic and the snap of a Basie cassette the opening clicked into instant conviviality. James greeted friends at the door, then, as the room became crowded, drifted with Inez (who had indeed worn her hat), watching people look at the drawings and prints wondering what they were and why they were all in black and white. When people asked James he told them, but most read the handout, nodded, and let it go. Contrary to expectation, the nudes were most popular, especially those of Gloria. He explained her medallion several times.

Joan looked great tending bar. She wore her hair just as she had in the several studies he had done that August which now hung beside her on the wall. Vaguely Pre-Raphaelite, they generally pictured her in the act of sorrowful contemplation, her splendid hair down, her blouse slightly open. She had come back from the festivale early to work for the maintenance department, earning money and getting an even tan while he tinkered in the cool of the basement, whistling along to AM radio. Evenings were spent together reading, going on walks, and drinking beers. It had been a good quiet time. They squabbled over everything and enjoyed each other enormously; they had long since decided to live near each other after college.

Field sports had been canceled due to rain, so that soon the small room was crowded. The scotch held up well under Joan's expert supervision; the gallery women made a considerable dent in the leftover wine but had also seen to it themselves that they were in no danger of ever running out. Almost everyone had dressed up; even some of his old friends from the lacrosse team dropped in for a nip before dinner. Carol came briefly, congratulated Joan on her portraits and insisted that someday James do one of her. Count Basie played; people ate cheese and talked loudly; James answered questions and told the several stories he had about receiving a free lunch. His friends in dramatic arts looked on in envy and admiration as he explained that when he worked outside strangers had often bought him lunch, simply for being an artist. Once it had been felafel at Amir's on 113th and Broadway, he explained, and the other two times souvlaki from a stand.

Joan smiled wryly.

"Art for lunch," Inez said reasonably.

Since he had only taken one course with a professor other than Dick Merisi, James was curious how they would approach the opening, and what they would say once there. He had of late seen very few art professors. Though he had long since satisfied his requirements in the major, he felt somewhat guilty for not doing an honors thesis in art. An August in the fine arts building, with all its very strange politics, had convinced him of the impracticality of such an endeavor. In any case real life (Joan, graduation, a job, a salary, a real business suit) was suddenly more of an adventure, promising as it did the grown-up satisfactions so missing at college and over the last summer. A real kitchen, a real bedroom, a real choice about where to go for dinner. Art could not satisfy as these things did; even this strangely grown-up day was an exception to the rule.

When he had first arrived at Amherst in midsummer he had been rather upset about Merisi's death and the imperviousness of the department to any form of rebuke. Now he felt less so. Merisi was, after all, famous; one of his paintings had been bought by the Wadsworth Athenaeum and his life story featured in *Art in America* and the *Times Arts and Leisure*. The department had trouble enough of its own; while admittedly shameless, its professors were at least now less comfortable.

They began to arrive. Shoulders squared, jaw set, hair perfect, Pike stood at the far end of the gallery, entertaining his two comrades, Williams and Poole. Pike, the magnetic lecturer popular among undergraduates and renowned for his ability to draw small but consistent numbers of unsuspecting women into the department, had come out of the Merisi investigations smelling like a rose. His classes remained large; he was still an asset to the otherwise plodding group of lecturers. He still wept regularly during lectures; while his tendencies to quote at length from Proust and the King James Bible as the lunch bell rang made some grumble, others, passing notes and sipping diet cola, enjoyed every minute and afterward praised him to the skies. He was taking an active role in planning the underground art annex, which meant among other things that he was still ignoring his advisees.

"For a man whose whole professional life hinges on minute niceties of perception and judgment," Joan said, joining him, "he seems to have a lot of fun at parties."

"I just pray he doesn't start talking about basketball again," Inez replied. "We spent half of Impressionist day in Intro to Art talking about Larry Bird."

But James had to agree. He could not dislike the man who had driven his professor to suicide; it did not suit either his long range sensibility or the immediate occasion. He went over to say hello.

Pike looked better at a distance than close by; as James approached, the highly expressive features became increasingly grotesque. Even so he could not but smile at the reddened, overly flared nostril wings, the thick oily eyebrow tufts, the bulging, pink-rimmed eyes. At auditorium distance, so effectively illuminated by greenish lecture light, the professor had evoked medieval damnation as effectively as his art; but now this pudgy man in shiny shoes seemed only odd, the sort one avoided at office parties.

His face had grown flabbier and paler since James had won the fellowship; had, in fact, begun to resemble, in corpulent meanness and strangeness of hue, that of a fifteenth-century

Flemish donor portrait. Conveniently pious, ruthlessly ambitious, pettily stature conscious: a surly Flemish merchant, that was all. But at least those eyes, ice-blue among yellowed, bloodshot whites, still lurked, cornered, the eyes of a small, feral, perhaps rabid forest creature. Something in them inspired apprehension if not real fear; quick and perceptive as ever, they maintained in this company an appearance as flat and chill as glass.

James welcomed him; Pike said a word about the number of people at the opening, then fell silent. James expressed his regret over the eviction. Pike nodded and at last said, "We'll have geraniums and palms in the new building, just like this someday. It looks very nice, all of it. I see you have some St. André."

"Right in the center. I couldn't resist," James replied. "It's my very favorite."

He slipped back to Joan while Pike ate.

At the other entrance (beyond Inez in her hat, dispensing scotch and discussing career plans with several younger actors) he saw Professor Williams with shadowy Grace Emily Poole, the untenured art historian who had succeeded Dick Merisi in his position. He went over. The two were discussing Merisi's work, for Grace had just seen the show in New York. While Grace was likable she very evidently had a nose for politics; it was here, more so than art history, that one suspected her real abilities to lie. She was often with Williams or Pike; today was no exception.

"So what did you think, Grace?" Williams asked, suppressing a smile.

"Terrible . . . wonderfully terrible," she said. ". . . all of them."

Her large eyes looked from Williams to James without blinking. In his course with her the previous semester, he had noticed that she was perpetually and inexplicably shrouded, as now, by the odor of scorched coffee. A diminutive woman, pale and oddly shaped, she was distinguished by prominent breasts well displayed, above which her eyes (their papery lids colored lavender and mauve) seemed permanently still and unblinking; seemed, in fact, the eyes of some Boschian nymphet, sensually expressive, damply amphibious. Her small, gesticulating hands, fluttering in half-light, revealed, when at rest, slender, semitranslucent fingers, ending in with exquisitely tapered, slightly curved, pearly-white nails. A wrought silver chain set with lusterless yellow gems sat heavily upon protruding collarbones; her yellow-green eyes loomed above them in the darkness, burning bright with their peculiar combination of (one felt encouraged to intuit) apprehension and hysteria.

"Terrible," she again sighed, somewhat hopefully.

James smiled. Though he dared not say it, he wished her good luck getting tenure, and good luck when she got it. She had a fair chance. As the first woman professor in a notorious department she would most likely need it, although just now she seemed right at home.

Professor Williams' gaze now rested upon Grace's disproportionate and unrestricted bosom. Grace, unblinking and self-assured as a reference librarian over her *OED*, bore his gaze with impunity, knowing through it, James sensed, both her triumph and her shame.

"I think some of his work is very fine," Williams said, winking at James.

James said, "Extraordinary. We won't see his like again."

Williams looked carefully at James, then turned back to Grace.

"Can you really have thought them *terrible*?"

Grace looked up. "Well, no. I meant—"

"What?"

"I suppose I was overwhelmed."

"Victim of your own passions?"

She considered without blinking.

"It's a living."

The gallery grew so noisy it was hard to hear people talk; the humid air grew close, saturated with damp exhalations of peanuts, cheese, and scotch. James, almost as red as Johnny Walker himself, had long since decided he was at just another Amherst cocktail party, a little world of its own that was whole and right and neat, where nice food and good clothes and witty conversation excused itself with ease before the troubling contradictions modestly matted, framed, and signed on the surrounding walls. He was part of it and enjoying it. Between different conversations with beautiful women he opened a window for air and chanced to look out at the rain on the quad.

The windows were slightly steamed; in the fading light of the spring afternoon, he saw the reflection of himself and the people behind, everyone set off by stark walls and simple art, everyone chatting in good clothes, looking mature. Stubby and Francis were dashing in ties; Carol looked good as always; Joan and Inez and the drama-ramas snapped their fingers, humming to "Basie Jam." A nice party, even if dancing was not allowed in the gallery. Even so, he could hardly wait for it to be over, so that, cleaning up, he and Joan could chat together alone, perhaps collapse on a bench to discuss in detail all that had happened.

He squinted, and past the reflection outside saw the quad —the rain-blackened trees, the mud puddles, the bright green of early spring sitting lightly, almost like a mist, over muddy ground, the freshmen walking in yellow slickers, carrying bags heavy with notebooks and work. The world was enormously beautiful.

Pike and Williams and Poole stood at the center of the room, surveying the art, speaking with unusual animation among themselves. They had said nothing about the prints or drawings so far. Joan tapped him.

They backed up to hear what was said. Grace Poole's voice stood out clear and somewhat whiny above the rest.

"One nineteen to one-oh-four," she said. "How about those Celtics?"

"How indeed," said Joan, with a quick kiss on the ear.